Dark Secrets

A Legacy of Memories from 1939 Sweden

A Novel

Mark,
Enjoy the Read!
Sher Davidson

Sher Davidson

outskirts
press

To my family, both here in the United States and in Sweden

PROLOGUE
SWEDEN, JULY 1939

The sky turned blood red as the sun set over Helga Johansson's family farm in southern Sweden. She peered out her bedroom window at the fields and beyond, to the dark Blekinge woods. Her five-year-old daughter, Sofia, played at her feet, babbling to her rag doll. Helga turned away from the window and began to pack her carpetbag for the long journey back to her home in America. It was late summer, just two days since the unspeakable had happened. She would end her visit to her homeland earlier than planned. She felt her emotions rise in her throat. She wanted to cry as she reflected on all that had happened since her return: meeting Rebecca, her brother Johann's wife, her beautiful Polish Jewish sister-in-law; discovery of her other brother Gunnar's dark activities in a neighboring village and of his six-year-old son. There were fun times, when Rebecca and Johann performed violin duets in the parlor nights during her visit, long walks with Rebecca, sisterly chats over their embroidery projects. It had been ideal in the beginning, and then all turned dramatically dark with Rebecca's unexplainable death and the incident. She would try to erase the horror of it from her memory she thought as she gulped back her tears and continued to pack.

● ● ●

Along with her oldest brother, Johann, still grieving the loss of his wife, Helga arrived at the docks in Malmö to board a ship bound for America for the second time in her life. She carried her carpetbag and a hard leather violin case. Johann held the small hand of her daughter, Sofia. As the three approached the ramp that led to the ship's deck, Johann cleared his throat and said, "Well then, Helga, we will both try to forget, won't we? You'll go back to Olaf and your life in America. All will be well."

Awkwardly, he tried to embrace her with his one free arm.

"Yes, Johann, but—"

Johann raised his hand to his lips. "We promised each other, remember? Don't worry. I'll be okay, busy raising Gunnar's son, Adolf. I intend to change his name to Axel, for reasons I know you will understand. He will help fill the empty place in my heart that Rebecca once occupied."

Helga let out a suppressed sob. "Johann, I will not forget her." She looked down at the violin case she carried. "I will always remember the beautiful music you both played for me, before she—"

"Don't say it, Helga—please."

The ship's horn let out a loud blast.

"Well, it's time, Helga. We will write to one another. Send me photos, when you can, of you and little Sofia; Olaf, too. Tell him I look forward to seeing some of those big fish he catches."

Johann leaned down to the small girl, whose hand he still held, and kissed her light-blonde-haired head, then handed her over to her mother. Helga struggled to hold her hand, the violin case, and the carpetbag, too.

The ship's porter, who stood near the boat ramp, reached out to help.

"Here, madam, I'll take your things and put them in your cabin. What is the number, please?"

Johann handed the man Helga's ticket.

"*Tack*," Helga said.

Johann turned to walk away, hesitated, then turned back to Helga to brush her cheek with a kiss, and quickly retreated with long strides to disappear into the crowd on the dock.

"Welcome aboard, Madam," said the captain at the ramp's entry. "Watch your step."

Helga brushed aside a tear from her cheek, took little Sofia's hand, and proceeded up the ramp.

● ● ●

The night before the ship was to arrive in the harbor in New York, Helga awoke with a scream. She sat up in bed, wiped the sweat from her forehead, cleared her sore throat as she glanced over at young Sofia, who sat up with fear in her eyes and began to cry.

"Don't worry, Sofia. Mama just had a bad dream. Now go back to sleep. Here's your doll. Tuck her in with you and have sweet dreams." Sofia lay back down as she clutched her rag doll close to her chest. The doll was a gift, made by Johann's wife, Rebecca.

There was a tap at the door.

"*Ya*, who's there?" Helga called out.

A voice on the other side of her door replied, "Are you alright, Ma'am? I heard a scream come from your cabin."

Still shaken by her own shriek, Helga replied, "Oh, ya, I'm sorry. Just a bad dream. I hope I've not woken others."

The voice on the other side of the door replied, "No, ma'am, I think they're all asleep. I'm a ship's steward on night duty. I was just walking around to check on the safety of our passengers and heard what sounded like a scream. Good night now."

Helga breathed a sigh of relief, then turned to Sofia who, still clutching her rag doll, looked up at her with frightened eyes.

"Now, please go back to sleep, Sofia." Helga tucked the blankets around her small daughter and soon Sofia, with her thumb in her mouth, was fast asleep.

● ● ●

Two days later, as their ship pulled into the docks in New York, Helga readied herself and Sofia for their arrival. She threw her carpetbag over her shoulder, the bag she had brought on her first trip to America so many years before, when she first immigrated. She made sure she had her train ticket handy in the interior pocket of her coat, then grabbed the violin case in one hand and Sofia's hand in her other one to descend the ramp to the dock.

"Excuse me," said Helga to a young man who

seemed to be directing passengers as they scurried here and there. "Where do I find a taxi to the train station, please?"

"Over there, ma'am." He pointed to a long row of yellow taxis near the dock. "I can help you with your things. You have your hands full."

The five day's train travel across the country was filled with pointing out sights to Sofia through the train windows, wobbly walks down the train-car aisles back and forth to the bathroom and dining car. Strangers commented on how cute the blonde-haired, blue-eyed little girl was, and Helga smiled with pride. She hesitated to talk much knowing some had trouble understanding her English, with her strong Swedish accent. She was self-conscious and anxious to avoid too much conversation, still in a state of shock from the events she would soon share with Olaf—or would she? She remembered the promise she made to Johann when he had cautioned her: "Try to forget it all, Helga. Don't even tell Olaf what has happened. It's best that way. It's our secret." In the end, she had agreed. She would keep her promise to Johann. It would forever remain their dark secret.

Helga and Sofia finally arrived in Portland, Oregon, where Olaf was to meet them. As the train pulled into Union Station, Helga peered out the window to see if she could see Olaf on the platform waiting for them. Oh, yes, there he was, his black fisherman's cap in his hand, waving to her as she stepped off the train with Sofia's hand in hers.

"Papa," Sofia called as she pulled away from Helga and ran towards the outstretched arms of Olaf.

Helga hung back, struggling with her heavy

carpetbag, her purse, and the violin.

Olaf approached now, with Sofia on his shoulders, leaned to brush Helga's cheek with a quick, almost shy, kiss. "Ya, ya, good to have you back, Helga, and the child. Missed you both. Here, let me take that," he said as he took the carpetbag and violin from Helga's hands.

Helga nodded with a smile.

The three made their way through the throng on the station platform to the old blue Ford flatbed truck, the one Olaf used to transport his fish to market. It always smelled of fish. Helga had gotten used to that.

"Are you hungry? Our neighbor Sonia made us a picnic lunch of pumpernickel sandwiches with bratwurst. I have some coffee in a thermos and juice for the little one."

"*Gut*," said Helga. "Let's eat it at a park before we start back to the coast, can we?"

"Ya, that's a good idea." Olaf helped Helga up into the truck, then handed Sofia to her to hold on her lap.

"What's this, a violin? A gift from Johann?" Olaf looked down at the case he had taken from Helga's hands.

"Ya, I will tell you about it later, Olaf. Let's go."

Olaf put Helga's things in the back of the truck, in the old wooden box with the hasp lock, where he usually kept nets, tools, flotsam and jetsam. He jumped up to the driver's seat and started the motor.

"Had the truck fixed while you were gone, Helga. She runs well now. Sorry for the smell. Fishing has been good lately."

"Gut," said Helga. She smiled at Olaf.

Lost in thought now as they drove from the train station to the big park on the hill, Washington Park, where they would stop to have their lunch before continuing to Astoria, Helga remembered something.

"I'll show you some photos of my family and my trip when we get home. Johann gave me a picture album with some nice photos he took during my visit. Hanna, their housekeeper, took a few also of the family and of our little Sofia. You will like them."

Olaf nodded and smiled as he turned into the park entrance.

Helga felt thankful she had the leather album Johann had given to her the night before she left. It would be the one thing that she would hold onto of her past, of her family farm in Sweden, of Johann and Rebecca, all she wished to remember. She would try to forget the rest.

Sofia continued, "This neighborhood was established in the 1880s, Lena, when hundreds of Finnish, some Danish and Swedish, immigrants arrived to fish the mouth of the Columbia and to work in the canneries or as lumberjacks, felling the big forests just north of the Columbia River in Washington. Fortunately for Helga and Olaf, their house remained standing after the Great Fire of 1922. Grandfather Olaf was a successful fisherman. When weather got too bad to fish, he worked at the Fishermen's Cooperative Packing Company, owned by our neighbor Mr. Lundberg. At the end of 1941, World War II was raging, and the US decided to stand with its allies. President Roosevelt sent American troops to stave off Hitler's threats to take over Europe. My father Olaf enlisted."

Sofia stopped for a moment as tears came to her eyes. Grandmother Helga appeared at the open door and interrupted Sofia and Lena's conversation. She wiped her hands on her apron and continued the story.

"Ya, that's true, Lena, what your mother is telling you. Your grandfather felt he had to show his patriotism to his adopted country, America. That was it, and I had little to say. Poor man, he died in a battle in France. I was left to fend for myself and to bring up your mother as best I could. She was only seven at the time. Ya, life was hard, Lena, but I managed to get by, housecleaning for the rich who lived in those upper-class neighborhoods, in Upper Town, you know, near the Evangelical Lutheran Church. I had lots of friends at the church who helped me. Oh, did we have fun at the Scandinavian festivals and community events. I sent your mother to the local elementary school. Life wasn't easy, but I managed—made me stronger."

Lena interrupted her grandmother's chronicles of the past and said, "I bet, Mama, you were as sad as Grandmother, sad as I am not to have a father."

Before Sofia could answer, Helga continued, "Your mother was a senior in high school when she fell in love with your father, her first beau, Eric Larsson. I never liked the boy much—reminded me too much of my younger brother, Gunnar, but that's another story. Your mother and father married right after graduation. Like my good husband, Olaf, Eric was a fisherman. I missed my friend Marta and decided it was time to go back to Chicago to visit her. I told Sofia and Eric they could live in our house, Olaf's and mine. Good thing, too, for your mother could never have managed to survive if it weren't for this big old house. My friends made sure she had business."

Lena sensed some bitterness in Grandmother's words and felt nervous. She began to bite her nails. Grandmother pushed her hand away from her mouth. "Lena, don't bite your nails; you'll make them bleed." Then, after a pause, she said, "Your mother could sew, as you know. She became the most popular dressmaker in town—even made dresses for the hoity-toity rich women on the hill."

Sofia got up from the couch swing and turned towards the door. "Well, that reminds me I have to get back to work. You two can continue talking."

After a brief pause, Helga said, "Lena, your father went missing at sea in a storm one winter night, and he never came back. You, my dear Lena, were born on February 10, 1953. You were just one month old at the time of this tragedy. Your father never knew the little jewel he had. We've been a good household of women ever since." Grandmother rose now from the swing. "Well, I have to get back to my pumpernickel bread, Lena. You can come and help me get the loaves out of the oven."

Chapter 2

As Lena looked back to her childhood, she realized how much she missed not having a father. It was an absence that affected much of her young life. She longed to be like other children in the neighborhood who she had watched riding on their father's shoulders or playing ball with them in the street. Added to that feeling of being different from the others was having a Grandmother who often screamed at night. She sometimes wondered if the neighbors heard those loud outcries.

One winter day Grandmother and Lena sat at the kitchen table peeling apples for apple dumplings when Lena finally got up the courage to ask about her father.

She knew Grandmother was thinking about him, too, in their conversation about the past a few weeks before; it seemed to Lena that they were always talking about the past.

Grandmother paused, picked up her knife again to begin paring another apple. Lost in thought as the apple peel unwound itself like a memory, she said,

"Well, Lena, our family seems to have lost its men to war and sea. As I've told you, your father was killed in a winter storm off the bar of the Columbia River. He should never have been out there, but he was a stubborn young man."

At that moment, Lena's mother came into the room for a cup of coffee and sat down with them at the kitchen table, with its blue-and-white checkered tablecloth.

Grandmother continued, "As I've already told you, your mother and Eric married too young, right out of high school. Well, that was not so good. She went and got herself pregnant with you, Lena. You were already in your mother's belly."

Sofia stood up from the table and went to the sink to wash out her cup, turning her back on the conversation. Lena could see her stiffen. She knew her mother never liked when Grandmother talked about her father that way.

She then turned abruptly to face Grandmother and Lena. "Mother, please," she said, her voice cold and sharp. "That wasn't necessary."

"Well, Sofia, the girl's got to know the story sooner than later."

Lena felt sorry for her mother that day, when she brought her apron to her face to wipe the wetness away, then rushed out of the room. Lena became even more curious about her grandmother's past: What made her hurt her daughter? She seemed so bitter at times.

Grandmother continued on this track even after Mother rushed from the room. She seemed hell-bent on Lena knowing the family story, at least the one here, but not what happened in Sweden in 1939, the time that was in the picture album. Why wouldn't she share more of that time, about her brothers and Rebecca, the sister-in-law she was so fond of? Those questions nagged at Lena. Mrs. Olsen, her English teacher, said a good writer had to "dig deep" to find answers they sought about their characters, even fictional ones.

That night, before Lena went to bed, Sofia brushed Lena's hair in front of the big oval dressing table mirror in Sofia's bedroom. The two looked at each other in the mirror. Hesitating for a moment, and then getting up her courage, Lena asked her mother to tell her more about her father. In the mirror's reflection, Lena could see Sofia's expression change from a smile to a look of sadness. Her mother's eyes glazed over, as if she were remembering her time with Eric—surely not all bad, Lena thought. The two were quiet for a minute and then Sofia said:

"Well, Lena, the sea can be relentless, without heart. I lost your father to the unforgiving Pacific Ocean, and my father to a war. Your grandmother and I have had to be strong. I know Grandmother can be difficult at times, but she is a model of strength for me."

Sofia set down her hairbrush, began to hum as she patted Lena's shoulder. "Now run along and get into your pajamas. You have school tomorrow."

Chapter 3

When Lena did well in English, wrote in her journal and told Grandmother she aspired to be a writer, Grandmother would say, "Lena, you're a smart girl, better to study something practical, like bookkeeping, or become a teacher. You can help take care of your mother then. I won't be here forever, you know."

Lena turned up her nose at that idea and from then on avoided talking about her love of literature and writing with her grandmother. Instead she buried herself in her books—novels, like *Gone with the Wind* and the classics like *Pride and Prejudice* by Jane Austen. It was her English teacher, Mrs. Olsen, who encouraged her to read all of Austen's books and those by the Brontë sisters, too. One of Lena's favorites was J.D. Salinger's *Catcher in the Rye*. She understood little about boys and the book aroused her interest and curiosity. Lena lived and breathed through the characters of the books she read and often wrote poems about them. Another of her favorite pastimes was drawing. Whenever she could, she escaped to her secret place out back under the wooden porch. Her cat, Pumpkin, would curl up on her lap while Lena rested her sketchbook on his back—he didn't seem to care. When it was warm enough, Lena would sit under the big old apple tree and draw pictures of her surroundings, of Pumpkin, or of Grandmother hanging out the laundry, their old house with the sloping back porch, whatever she could see that drew her eye. Then she would write a poem about her picture.

In the winter, when it was overcast and drizzly, Grandmother became taciturn and crotchety. She wouldn't talk much and her screams at night occurred more frequently. Lena could hear her mother, who was almost always more cheerful, humming one of her favorite songs under her breath, songs like *Blue Moon*, from the 1940's, as she sewed. Lena would mope around the house, trying to avoid Grandmother's commands.

Sofia sometimes looked up from her sewing and said, "Lena, why don't you go and help your grandmother in the kitchen and don't talk a lot. She'll be fine. She's maybe just remembering her past. Be patient with her."

Lena tried, but she could not understand Grandmother's mercurial nature, her mood swings and nightly screams. She grew restless and didn't sleep well. Grandmother seemed to have a tormented soul, which Lena was too young to understand.

Shy, Lena didn't have any friends. Sometimes her loneliness had a type of gravity that felt like it would crush her. Grandmother's nightmares didn't help. Lena was always tired, but then she would leave the house and go for a walk, look out from their hill over the Astoria Bridge, and promise herself, under her breath, that someday she would leave all this behind, cross that bridge and see the world and have adventures of her own.

Other days she would walk down the hill to the beach where the gulls would glide in like paper airplanes, cawing, crying out for food as they flew in swirls around her. She threw bread crumbs from her pockets to them. One day she spotted something on the beach, in the distance—something small and white but not stationary. It moved ever so slightly, and the big gulls swooped in to peck at it. As Lena came closer, she realized it was a young gull, deformed, with just one leg. The other gulls were pestering it. Lena dropped to the sand to try to help, but all the gulls surrounded her and continued to peck and pester the small, deformed gull. As they swooped down around her, Lena felt how she did when Grandmother heckled her and said things like, "Lena, do this, do that, wear this, stand up straight," and she wondered if she could ever just be herself, as imperfect as she was, like the small, deformed gull?

Chapter 4

A thick blanket of fog unfurled itself slowly, stealthily, like a cat, over Astoria. It rolled in from the Pacific over the Long Beach Peninsula, across the Astoria Bridge to settle itself there for the night. Foghorns sounded from time to time when maritime vessels slipped by the port. On the beach, a lone person wandered aimlessly, as small fishing craft bobbed up and down in the ink-black bay. A few lights twinkled throughout the mostly sleeping city. All was still.

Sixteen-year-old Lena Larsson woke with a start. Not as usual, from her Grandmother Helga's screams in her sleep, but to a deep silence, like in a dream. She sensed something was wrong and turned over in bed to listen. She couldn't hear a thing, not even the sound of her grandmother's heavy snoring. She got up, pulled on her pink slippers, the ones Grandmother had knitted, and walked down the hall past her mother's room to her grandmother's. The door was ajar. She peeked in. Startled to see the bed was empty and Helga's peach chenille robe missing, as well as her ragged felt slippers, the ones with the backs turned down, she ran to her mother's room and cried out, "Mama, Mama, Grandmother's gone!"

Sofia sat up in bed, alarmed, her long greying hair tangled around her neck as she brushed wisps of it from her eyes.

"Lena, whatever are you doing up so late and walking around? What do you mean, she's gone? For heaven's sake, you must be dreaming. Now go back to bed."

"No, Mama," cried Lena. "Grandmother's not in her bedroom—she's gone somewhere."

Mother dragged herself out of bed, slipped on her blue terrycloth robe, pulled her hair back in a knot and slipped a tortoiseshell comb into it—the one Helga had given her. She hurried across the hallway to Helga's room. Lena followed.

"Oh, my god, where could she be? We must call the police—but wait. She might just be out on the porch swing. She likes to go there when she can't sleep."

They ran down the stairs, then the hallway towards the front door. They could hear the sound of the screen door swinging against the doorframe.

"Someone has unlatched the outer screen door," said Sofia.

Strange—they always latched it at night. Grandmother insisted on that. The door made an eerie sound as it swung back and forth in the night's cold breeze. Lena peered out to the swing on their enclosed front porch, but Grandmother wasn't there. A cold ocean breeze swept up their hill, flowed in and made Sofia and Lena shiver. Lena twisted her robe belt in her hands and started biting her fingernails.

"Where do you think she could have gone, Mama?" Lena asked.

"I don't know, but I'd better call the police. Maybe she's just walking somewhere, dazed, can't find her way back home," said Sofia. "Lena, sit down on the parlor sofa and calm yourself. I'll call the police and then bring you some hot milk. Don't worry—we'll find Grandmother."

Lena did as she was told, curled up on the sofa and clutched one of the crochet-covered pillows Grandmother had made to her chest, frightened and worried. Sofia came back into the room with the milk and sat down next to her. They both shivered.

There was a loud knock at the door. Sofia jumped up to answer it. Lena followed. There, standing on the front porch, was Big Ollie—well, that's what everyone called Astoria's police chief. He was a big, gruff-looking Swede, but nice as an old teddy bear, Lena thought. When she was in grade school, he gave all the kids licorice sticks after his talk about safety.

Big Ollie looked serious as he stood there on the porch holding something. In the dim light, at first, Lena and Sofia couldn't make out what it was. Then, as their eyes adjusted, they saw he was holding a pair of slippers. He cleared his throat and said, "Good evening, Sofia. Do you recognize these?"

"Why, they're my mother's slippers," said Sofia. "For heaven's sakes, where did you find those?"

She took the damp slippers from Big Ollie's hands and clutched them to her breast. Tears began to well up in her eyes. In shock, Lena just stood there and watched and wondered what would happen next.

"Sofia, I'm sorry to say we found them on the beach,

sitting on the sand, as if someone just walked out of them towards the sea."

Sofia gasped. "No, she couldn't have."

"We've got the Coast Guard alerted," continued Ollie. "We have our people out searching on the beach, too. I'm sorry, Sofia, to have to report this to you. I'm sure we'll find her soon and everything will be okay."

To Lena, her mother didn't look so sure of that; shaking, she pulled her bathrobe tight around herself, sank down on the porch swing, and motioned Lena to sit by her. She pulled her daughter close.

"Mama, what's happened?" Lena asked. "Why did Grandmother leave her slippers on the beach?"

"I don't know, Lena," said Sofia, "but we'll find out soon enough. Now go inside. It's cold out here and you'll catch your death. Ollie, would you like to come in and have some coffee?"

"No thanks, Sofia." Big Ollie looked nervous as he twirled his black-and-white police cap around and around in his hand. "I'd better get back to the station. Have to check on what we hear from the searchers and the Coast Guard. I'll let you know as soon as I find out something."

"Okay. Thanks, Ollie. I'll wait to hear from you, the moment you find my mother," said Sofia.

"Good night now." Big Ollie put on his cap, nodded at Sofia and Lena, turned and trudged down the worn wooden stairs to the sidewalk. He walked quickly to the curb where his police car was parked.

Three days later, Sofia was informed that the Coast Guard had found Helga's body, still in her nightgown, dashed up on some rocks. She had taken her secrets with her.

Chapter 5

Helga's funeral was attended by many of the older Scandinavian friends who, shocked as they were by her suicide, tried to support her grief-stricken daughter and granddaughter. Flowers were sent to the house, and many of the local neighbors brought over home-baked bread, soup, sausages, herring, and fresh salmon.

When Sofia and Helga arrived home after the funeral, Sofia took off her worn coat and walked up the stairs, while Lena stoked the fire in the potbelly stove in the kitchen and let the tears fall down her cheeks. Finally, Sofia came downstairs and into the kitchen, holding something out to Lena. It was the brass box, the one where Grandmother used to keep her long hairpins and pretty tortoiseshell combs.

"Here, Lena," said Sofia. "I've put Grandmother's ashes in here. We'll take them to Sweden one day and bury them in the country where she was born."

Tearful, Lena collapsed into her mother's arms. With a sob, she said, "Do you think, Mother, we will ever know why Grandmother often called out in her sleep, and why she took her own life?"

"I don't know, Lena." Sofia 's pale blue eyes watered. She sat down at the kitchen table and rested her head on her folded arms and began to hum, under her breath. It was not a happy song, but the one played at the funeral. With her eyes closed, she rocked in her chair, ever so slightly—back and forth, humming.

After Grandmother's suicide, Mother and Lena seemed to crumple from within, like marionettes without their master to pull their strings. Grandmother Helga had been such a strong "captain of the ship," they now seemed listless without a rudder. They didn't talk much about the night of the suicide. It was as if they had bottled it up and put a cork on it.

Chapter 6

When Lena was a senior in high school, she entered the Senior class writing contest and won second place for a poem she wrote about her grandmother:

Into an Undersea World

At sea's edge an old woman walked
Alone, lost in painful memory
Waves washed in and out
In and out.

Moonlight waned as clouds drifted
Night was darker, colder now,
The woman stepped out of her slippers
Walked to the water's edge.

She slipped away from her sad memories
To the depths of the sea, where only
Beauty could be seen, to be held
In its warm embrace forever.

Mrs. Olson, Lena's English teacher remarked, "Lena, you're a fine writer. I was moved by the poem you wrote for last week's assignment. I noticed you alluded to the loss of your grandmother. I know about what happened—it was in the *Astoria Times*. I'm sure you know that. Sometimes, we can turn hard and sad events in our lives into beautiful writing. I encourage you to do that."

Lena came home that day and ran into the house to find her mother in her usual place, working at her sewing machine.

"Mother, Mother, Mrs. Olsen liked my poem. I won the Senior Class writing contest, well second place anyway. Mrs. Olsen said I may be able to enter a writing contest again next year at the Community College, one which the Rotary Club sponsors with the College. I could win a scholarship to go to the Sorbonne in France," Lena exclaimed. She was breathless from running up the old wooden front porch steps of their house.

Sofia looked up from her sewing in surprise. "That's wonderful, dear. But how can this be—you know that I'm not sure we can afford to send you to the college.

"Mother, Mlle Ragot, my French teacher, is helping me apply for a scholarship. She's sure I will get it. Then once I've completed my first year at the college, and if I win the contest, I could go for my sophomore year to study at the Sorbonne in Paris. I know Grandmother and you always wanted me to learn to speak more Swedish, but I'm so glad I like French better. Mademoiselle Ragot is one of my favorite teachers second to Mrs. Olsen. I'll have the summer to work on my writing before it has to be submitted and maybe I can get a part-time job, too."

Lena could see the pride in her mother's eyes. She worried about her mother. She knew she must have wished to do more in her life than just sit at a sewing machine, must have had other dreams. They'd never talked about that. Lena knew that Grandmother Helga had just expected her daughter to support the family with her talent for sewing.

Sofia looked up. "Lena, I'm so thrilled for you. Let's celebrate! I'll stop work on Mrs. Lundberg's dress right now." She set down her sewing and stood up. "How about going down to the Big Pink to have tea in their lovely dining room and maybe some pastry, too."

"Oh, could we, Mother?" Lena could hardly believe her ears—for her mother to stop work in the middle of the day and go out for tea; this was a rare occasion. She had never entered the Astor Hotel, so often called "the Big Pink" due to the color of its exterior paint. Maybe this was the beginning of a new era for Lena Larsson, and just maybe she would be able to sleep without waking up thinking she had heard a scream.

Chapter 7

One day Lena walked into Mother's sewing room with her journal and plopped down on the floor by her machine, looked up, and said, "I'm writing Grandmother's story . I might enter it in the contest next year if it comes out well enough. I need to understand why she had those terrible nightmares when she was alive and why she took her own life.

Sofia set down the garment she was working on, got up, walked to the window, and looked out. "Well, Lena, I think she did not start to scream at night until after she returned with me when I was only five, from a visit to Sweden in 1939, with her brothers, my uncles Johann and Gunnar. I often wonder what might have happened there—what sort of trauma."

"What do you think could have triggered dreams so bad they made her scream?" said Lena.

"Well, I'm not sure," said Sofia. "Her friend, Mrs. Lundberg, who lives next door told me that my father worried about her after my birth, as she was prone to depression. I was the second child she bore. She lost my sister to scarlet fever as an infant before I came along several years later. You remember I told you when you were a little girl that your name was very special? It's the name of my sister I never knew.

Oh, Mother," said Lena, "I always meant to ask you where you got my name. Is it a Swedish name?"

"Yes, it is. Grandmother was pleased with your father's and my choice. Well, to continue the story, by 1939, my father was doing pretty well in the fishing business, and he scraped together enough money for a ship's passage to Sweden from New York for your grandmother and me. Of course, she had to take the Union Pacific train across the country first. It must have been quite an adventure for her, traveling alone with only me, a small child. That was shortly before WWII and, as I've told you before, Lena, two years later your grandfather enlisted in the US Army and was killed in a battle in France. I was just seven at the time. Your grandmother suffered much trauma in her life."

"Maybe Grandmother screamed because she lost her husband to the war; maybe it was grief that caused her such anxiety, do you think?" said Lena.

"Well, I'm not sure. Like you, I grew up hearing your grandmother at least one night a week. At first, I thought it was because my father was killed in the war, but after Mrs. Lundberg told me that she remembered Grandfather had mentioned Helga's nightmares before he went into the army, I always sensed my mother had some deep, dark secret she wouldn't disclose from her visit to Sweden."

Lena reflected on the past she remembered.

There were days when Grandmother and Lena sat at the kitchen table, especially on the cold wintry days when it rained, and a gloom hung over everything like a damp fishing net. Helga would fix hot chocolate and the two would talk about Grandmother's Swedish past, what she remembered of it. For Lena, those were some of the best memories she had of her Grandmother. It was those times that Lena asked her Grandmother questions about her past, but then sometimes Helga would suddenly become angry and stomp out of the room. It was hard for Lena to understand Grandmother's moods. She always felt Helga held secrets deep inside herself she couldn't reveal. Now she related those times to her mother as she tapped her pencil on her notebook and talked to her mother.

Sofia nodded her head and pondered. "Yes, Lena, I remember, too, how your grandmother became angry when you asked too many questions, but why? What did she have to hide?"

"My favorite times were when she brought out her old leather-covered photo album" said Lena. "She would point to a few photos from her childhood on the farm in Skåne. I remember the photo outside the blacksmith shop, Grandmother standing next to her father, my great-grandfather. He looked so stern. Grandmother said he made her and her brothers work hard. She said that her favorite job was to take the horseshoes to the local farmers after her father finished forging them. She'd ride a horse. Did she ever tell you about that, Mother?"

Sofia laughed. "Oh, yes, many times. She loved that old mare. She named her Oats, *Havre* in Swedish, because she ate so much. Apparently, her father was a stern man and very hard on her brothers, Johann and Gunnar, but your grandmother always thought she was his favorite. He did give her opportunities to ride the mare when he wanted her to make deliveries for him. He also brought her books. Like you, she loved to read."

"Yes, but she said they were boring books he got from the pastor at the Lutheran church," said Lena.

Sofia smiled and, for a moment, looked distant, then said, "Oh, yes, she told me about those boring church books, but she was lucky and met a girl named Sofia—she named me after her—who came from a more cultured family than Grandmother's. Apparently, Sofia traveled to England often with her mother, and she'd lend Helga some of the books she brought back. That helped Mother learn English. I remember one of them was *Wind in the Willows*. Do you remember I read that to you when you were a child?"

"Oh, yes, of course I do. I loved that story," said Lena. "Sometimes when Grandmother showed me photos in her old leather album there were a few missing, I could tell because the sticky stuff from the corner tabs that once held them in place was still there, and the squares were less faded than the rest of the page. She always became agitated when I asked her where those photos were and why she had removed them. I remember one night when you were at choir practice at the church, Mother, and Grandmother and I were at home. She did begin to open up a bit with me. We sat by the woodstove in the kitchen, warming our hands. Grandmother was knitting. She let the ball of yarn drop from her lap where Pumpkin liked to play with it. Grandmother started to talk about the Lundbergs, and how kind they were to her and Grandfather Olaf."

"You know, Lena, your grandparents were very poor when they first came to Astoria. All they had to eat sometimes, if your grandfather was lucky and didn't have to sell his whole catch to the canneries, was a slab of fish and some brown bread your grandmother baked if they could afford the flour. Your grandmother said, at least, all the neighbors pitched in and helped each other. She often said they could not have made it if it wasn't for the help of the Lutheran church ladies and the *Fralsninggarmen*, the local Salvation Army. She loved to buy the old secondhand furniture there and kitchen stuff. Why, half this house is furnished from that place. Even her old blue-and-white enameled kettle—you remember the one, Lena—is from the Salvation Army."

Sofia paused and walked back to her sewing machine, then looked at Lena and said, "As hard as it might be, I think it's time we finally go into her room. It's time we clean out her things and gather up her clothes to give to Goodwill for the poor people in Finn Town, who could use them. Maybe we'll find something there that will give us some answers—and just maybe help you sleep better, also."

Chapter 8

It was a gloomy winter day. Sofia turned the dented brass doorknob to Grandmother's old room slowly, with some trepidation, not knowing what they might find. It had been nearly two years since Helga's suicide. Her room had remained closed and locked. Neither Sofia nor Lena could bear to enter, knowing it would bring back painful memories. Now the time had arrived. Sofia hoped to rent the room out to a boarder, which would help with their expenses and provide money for Lena to continue her education.

There was a faint whiff of the rose-water scent that Grandmother used to sprinkle on everything, including herself. The window shades were drawn, and the room was dark and damp. At first, Lena wanted to run out, as tears came to her eyes and memories of Grandmother Helga flooded her. Sofia also wiped aside her tears and then began her usual humming under her breath. The lace curtains Grandmother had made for her windows were grey with dust, as was her old wicker rocking chair. The porcelain figurine of the milkmaid with the duckling she had brought from Sweden sat on a side table. Lena brushed past the rocking chair and it began to move back and forth slowly—as if Grandmother sat there watching them.

"Let's get some light in here, Lena. Your grandmother hated the long, overcast times in Astoria, when the sun didn't shine for days, like in Sweden."

As she said this, Sofia began to raise the yellowing, slightly torn, old paper shades. A streak of sun came through the clouds and shown a light on the floor of the room—as if Helga's spirit was showing them the way. At least, that's what Lena later wrote in her journal.

"I remember Grandmother always telling me she loved the summers best, when we had sunshine and could go on our beach picnics. Do you remember that?" asked Lena.

"Oh, yes, of course, dear—we did have fun on those picnics, didn't we?" Sofia laughed. "Remember how your Grandmother Helga would pack up our big wicker picnic basket, fill it with her delectable pastries, pumpernickel bread, and herring, which I know you didn't like much, gouda cheese, apples, and tangerines, your favorite fruit. We'd head for the beach. Grandmother always insisted she wear those old blue-striped bloomers and the puffy-sleeved top she called her 'bathing attire.' What I loved most was when she'd top it off with that old captain's hat that had belonged to my father. Remember that, Lena?"

Lena smiled and said, "Yes, those were happier times, weren't they, Mother?"

Sofia nodded with a vague smile on her face, then said, "Well, let's get to work and see what we can find here, Lena."

They began with the closet. Sofia hummed softly as she sorted the clothing that she removed from the wire hangers and then handed to Lena to fold. It was Lena's job to place them in the big yellow paper bags they had picked up from the Goodwill store. When they had finished emptying the closet, they went to the dresser and began to empty the drawers of Grandmother's underwear, slips, and sweaters, many which she had knitted herself. Finally, the bottom drawer was the last one to be opened. That's the one where Grandmother kept her old leather-covered album, the one Lena had so often pored over with her, the one with the photos from Sweden.

As Sofia leafed through the album, she took care not to tear the thin tissue sheets that protected the dark chocolate-colored pages. She paused a moment over a few of the photos, like the one of her as a little girl, the one where the small boy, Axel, was handing her the daisies, and then closed the album and handed it to Lena.

"Well, Lena," Sofia said, "I guess we'll have to find a special place to keep this. Someday you'll want to share it with your own children." She set the album in the other cardboard box they had carried into the room. Under where the album had lain, they discovered a letter and three more photos wrapped in a linen handkerchief, with a forget-me-knot flower embroidered on the corner.

Mother carefully unfolded the handkerchief and exclaimed, "Look, Lena! Grandmother wrote a letter." Sofia's hand trembled as she handed the letter to Lena. "It's for you. You should read it first."

Lena took the thin paper envelope that had the words "For My Granddaughter" written on the outside.

She lifted up the unglued flap and carefully pulled out the letter to read:

Dear Lena,

I want you to have something to remember me by. I had very little from the old country, when I returned with your mother, then only 5 years old—only the photo album and the violin that had belonged to Rebecca. Johann said she would want me to have it. Later, at the end of the war, her father's friend, Saul, who survived the holocaust by a miracle, wrote, not knowing Rebecca was deceased, and said that her father played his violin to help the others in the camp feel better—he played for long hours at a time, until they took him to the gas chambers. Johann handed Rebecca's violin, in its case, to me as I was about to board the ship that would take my small daughter, your mother, Sofia, and me back to America. I have decided to leave these two things to you, granddaughter, and to take my own life. I can no longer live with the painful memories of the horrible event that happened in Sweden just before the war started.

Your loving grandmother, Helga

Mother's hand came to her mouth and she let out a cry, "Oh, that must be the secret that your grandmother always hid from you, Lena—from me, too. At least, we now know, for sure, her nightmares were from some dark memory she had from her visit to Sweden. But what could she have experienced? What did she mean by 'the horrible event' and was it on the farm or in some other place? Much that was unspeakable was happening in Europe at the time. I know you said you studied the Holocaust in your history class. But it didn't take place in Sweden. I have such vague memories from that trip, when I was just five, but it seemed they were always happy ones, seeing my uncles and playing with a small boy, a few years older than me."

Lena shook her head, not knowing what to say and then exclaimed, "Look, Mother, she's left the three photos, the ones which were missing from the album, I suspect."

In faded ink on the back, in her shaky handwriting, Grandmother had identified the people in the photos. There was the one of Johann and his pretty wife, Rebecca. Another one was of Grandmother holding young Sofia. Next to her stood Rebecca, in a pretty flowered dress. There was also the small boy in the photo. He had a distant look in his eyes and was holding out to Sofia a bouquet of flowers—daisies, perhaps.

"Who do you think that little boy is, Mother?"

"I think that would be Axel, the son of Gunnar, Grandmother and Johann's brother. You remember the letter that Grandmother read to us from Johann in which he talked about Axel. He was born with a mental defect but was a 'sweet boy,' she would say. He would have been my cousin."

"I wonder why Grandmother didn't tell us more about Gunnar and the boy," Lena asked.

"Yes, it's strange, Lena. I found, when I asked about Gunnar, your grandmother became agitated, so I just avoided the subject. Now that she's gone, I have regrets I didn't ask more questions."

There was one more photo. It was of Helga, Rebecca, and Johann. In the shadows behind them stood a man who had a towhead like Lena's and deep-set angry eyes. When Lena pointed to him, her mother said, "That must have been Gunnar. We don't know much about him, do we? All Grandmother ever said was he went off to the war and died. This never made sense to me as Sweden didn't have a fighting military. They declared themselves a neutral nation in WWII. Strange." Sofia went on humming and gathering up Grandmother's things to put in the boxes.

"Why do you think she never wanted to talk more about them, her brothers and Johann's wife, Rebecca, Mother?"

"I don't know Lena. Someday, when you finish school, we must go together to Sweden and meet the family. Maybe we'll finally discover Grandmother's secret—perhaps the terrible thing that made her take her own life."

Sofia made a last sweep of the drawer with her hands. In the very back was the violin. Lena had never seen it, nor had her mother, but they remembered sometimes at night hearing Grandmother lightly pluck the strings. Then there would be silence, and finally, a loud sound as the dresser drawer was slammed shut. They guessed that Grandmother put the instrument back in its place, to perhaps forget the memories it evoked.

As she placed the violin case in the box, Sofia commented, "Too bad Grandmother didn't give this to you when she was alive, Lena. Maybe you could have taken lessons at school and played it for her. Sadly, your grandmother had many secrets we may never understand. She would often say to me, 'You know, Sofia, our lives are marked by sadness and loss.' I called the days she talked like that the dark days."

Sofia brushed a tear away from her cheek and went on humming as they finished cleaning up the room. "I guess I'll have to make a new coverlet for the bed and some pillow shams. We have a young woman coming to look at the room next week. She may be our boarder. Let's hope so. We have to start saving money for that trip we're going to take to Sweden together, Lena. Now, let's finish up and take these boxes and bags out to the front porch. Our neighbor, Mr. Lundberg, offered to pick them up and take them to the Goodwill. Then we'll go make supper and talk about your future writing career."

Lena loved when her mother made reference to her "future writing career"—it meant Mother took her seriously. She also loved it when she talked about their going to Sweden together one day. Just the thought of it made her days seem brighter.

As they left the room, Lena looked back once and then closed the door.

\

Chapter 9

One day, a week after Mother and Lena had cleaned out Grandmother's room, Mother asked Lena to drop off something she had found there to Mrs. Lundberg. She thought Mrs. Lundberg would appreciate the old magazine in which there was a photo of a group of women, the Swedish Ladies League. Mrs. Lundberg was pictured in the photo and someone, probably Grandmother, had drawn a circle around her face. Lena was glad to have an excuse to visit their neighbor, to ask her more about her grandmother. Maybe she could shed more light on her life, parts that Sofia and Lena didn't know.

Lena knocked at the door. No one answered. Then Lena rang the bell, one of those brass bells with a small handle that one turns to make it ring.

Mrs. Lundberg came to the door dressed in the same kind of dowdy dress that Grandmother used to wear, which they called a "housedress." Her hair was cut short in a bob now. She had on an apron and appeared to be wiping her hands on it.

"Oh, Lena, it's you. How delightful. I just finished baking some cookies, *pepperkaker*. Come in and have a cup of tea and a cookie with me."

"Well, Mrs. Lundberg, I can't stay long," said Lena, "but mother wanted me to drop off something we found in Grandmother's old room when we were cleaning it out last week. She thought you'd be interested."

A look of curiosity crossed Mrs. Lundberg's face. "Why, yes, why don't you show it to me. Come now. I have to get the last batch of ginger cookies out of the oven before they burn."

Lena set her backpack down in the hallway, pulled out the old magazine, careful not to rip its cover, brittle with age, and followed Mrs. Lundberg to the kitchen. The house was filled with the good smell of baking cookies. It brought back memories of when Grandmother was alive. Lena remembered how often she had come home to the same smells wafting out to the screened-in front porch.

"My, it's good to see you, Lena. You're growing up. In high school now, your mother tells me, and loving your English and French classes. She says you want to be a writer, a poet maybe. Is that right?"

"Oh, yes. I love history, too. In a way that's what I'd like to talk to you about."

Mrs. Lundberg looked puzzled for a minute, and then curious. "Sure, Lena, ask me anything you would like—I presume it may be about Goldie." She laughed. "I mean your grandmother, right?"

Lena knew that Grandmother's friends in Astoria called her Goldie, as her hair was, at one time, so golden-colored.

"Yes, but I should first give you this magazine," said

Lena as she handed the magazine to the older woman.

Mrs. Lundberg took the magazine and invited Lena to sit down. Lena pulled out the chair and sat down across from her neighbor at her maple kitchen table covered with a crocheted ivory tablecloth. Mrs. Lundberg glanced down at the magazine, leafing through its pages for a moment.

"Oh, my, this is an oldie. It's our Ladies League journal that we published once a year. I always tried to get your grandmother to join us, but she said she wasn't interested and didn't have the time for such frivolous things. Your grandmother wasn't one to mince words. I guess you know that."

"Well, yes, I guess I do," Lena said. She hesitated and took a sip of tea that Mrs. Lundberg poured for her. Then, feeling a bit nervous, she jumped in with her question.

"The thing I wanted to ask about was if my grandmother spoke to you often about her life in Sweden and especially about her brothers Johann and Gunnar?"

"Well, yes, she did. We shared a lot about our families. As you know, I'm Swedish, too. Your grandmother and I had that in common. Her father was a blacksmith and a farmer. My father was a businessman in Stockholm who saw the future was in America when he immigrated in 1898. I was born here, so I didn't always relate easily to those my age who came from the old country, but your grandmother and I had a special friendship ever since we became neighbors and helped each other survive the Great Fire of 1922. You know, Lena, tragedies can bring people together. My husband, like your grandfather, was in the fishing industry and ran the cannery where your grandfather sometimes worked during the off-season. Goldie—I mean Helga—was a dynamic young woman in those days and never failed to speak her mind. She loved to have Olaf's, fisherman friends stop by and taste her Swedish cookies or her warm bread just out of the oven. Oh, my, that reminds me, I have to get that last batch of cookies."

Lena loved hearing this story, a side of Grandmother she had never really witnessed. She thought to herself that things must have changed a lot for Grandmother once she came along and Grandmother had to help her mother raise a young child.

Mrs. Lundberg got up and opened the oven door, pulled out a baking sheet of delicious smelling cookies. She set the baking sheet down and slipped some cookies onto a white milk-glass dish.

"Would you like a couple, Lena?" asked Mrs. Lundberg as she set the plate on the table.

"Well, yes, if you're sure you have enough?"

"Of course, there's plenty and besides we have more to talk about, don't we? Go on with your questions," said Mrs. Lundberg as she sat down opposite Lena.

Lena continued with her questioning: "Well, I really need to know more about my grandmother's time in Sweden when she took my mother there to visit her brothers right before the Second World War."

"Yes, those were harrowing times in the world," said Mrs. Lundberg. "I was always surprised that your grandfather, Olaf, was willing to risk the danger your grandmother might encounter, traveling at that time. I think they were having some problems. Olaf told me that your grandmother was often depressed. He thought she was lonesome for her family back in Sweden and that the trip would do her good."

"But did she tell you much about her brothers she was going to visit?" Lena asked.

"Oh, my, yes. Well, at least about her brother Johann. She said he was a wonderful violinist who performed all over Europe. She was very proud of him. She didn't say a lot about the younger of her two brothers—I think his name was Gunnar. She did tell me that he was one of the reasons she immigrated, that he had done something unforgivable." Mrs. Lundberg hesitated. "Well, I can't seem to remember the details. It just seemed to me she was very afraid of that brother."

Lena's curiosity was piqued. "Oh, please do try to remember, Mrs. Lundberg. I need to know everything to try and understand why my grandmother screamed in her sleep and committed suicide. This may be a clue."

"Well, I think your Uncle Gunnar tried to rape his sister, your grandmother. I'm sure by now you've heard that word."

For a moment, Lena felt her face grow red with embarrassment. She had learned that word and what it meant from her reading, but admitted to herself, Mother and she had never discussed it.

Mrs. Lundberg went on: "Evidently, from what Goldie told me, your great-uncle Johann intervened at the time. She told me that it was Johann who encouraged her to immigrate to America, to leave their family home where he feared she had little future."

For a moment, as Lena remembered her grandmother's horrible screams in the night, she wondered if that incident with Gunnar was the sole cause of Grandmother's bad dreams. Something did not gel for her. She had a notion that it was something more. Lena sat in a kind of trance as she tried to absorb this new information. She pondered for a minute then looked up as Mrs. Lundberg went on.

"Your grandmother was just fifteen years old at the time, just a bit younger than you are now, Lena. Six months later she immigrated to America with her good Swedish friend Marta. I think that was her name. Goldie had a great deal of courage."

"I always thought that Grandmother had so many secrets. She never told me much about the younger of her two brothers. That he had done this terrible thing. It may explain why she never wanted to show me the photos of Gunnar, nor talk about him much," said Lena. "She must have lived with a great deal of fear and sadness. I can't imagine her even wanting to see him when she returned to Sweden."

"Well, I sort of felt the same way, Lena, and worried about her when she left to visit her brothers in 1939. She was gone for only three months in the late spring and early summer. Olaf didn't expect her home until the fall, but she came home earlier. For weeks she didn't wish to talk much about her voyage or her visit with her brothers. I didn't want to force her, but little by little, she told me a few details. Not much. You've probably heard most of them. I think the hardest thing for her was to accept the death of a woman she called Rebecca, her sister-in-law with whom she became very close in a short period of time."

Lena sat in a stupor as she munched on a cookie. In her head she was trying to put together all the new information, pieces of the puzzle of her grandmother's life.

"Lena, are you alright, dear? I hope what I told you hasn't upset you."

"Oh, no, not at all, Mrs. Lundberg. I appreciate the information. It just makes me sad to think of what Grandmother must have suffered."

Mrs. Lundberg looked down at her watch and stood up. "Oh, my, I'm afraid I have to get ready to meet my husband downtown now. You come by anytime you want, and we can talk about more pleasant things." She began to remove her apron.

"Oh, I'm sorry to stay so long, Mrs. Lundberg. Thank you for the cookie." Lena wiped the crumbs from around her mouth and stood up to walk down the hall for her backpack.

"Wait, Lena," said Mrs. Lundberg. She held out a plate of cookies.

"Here, bring these to your mother."

"*Tack*," Lena said.

Mrs. Lundberg smiled.

Lena thought to herself that she was sure Mrs. Lundberg was surprised she remembered any of the Swedish her grandmother had taught her. She threw her backpack over her shoulders, took the plate from Mrs. Lundberg's hand and walked out. "*Adyö!*"

Lena knew it would have pleased Grandmother to know that she was still practicing her Swedish even though she preferred French.

Chapter 10

After cleaning out her grandmother's room and learning more from Mrs. Lundberg, Lena still felt bewildered by her grandmother's nightmares and suicide. She spent many lonely hours pondering her childhood with Grandmother, trying to make sense of it. Without the distraction of friends her age, she became morose. Later, she wrote in her journal: "I don't know what I would have done if I hadn't met Yael, my first true friend, who has also become a kind of mentor to me. I met her in my senior year history class at Astoria High School. It was odd the way it happened. We were studying WWII and the Holocaust. Yael always asked the most interesting questions and seemed to know much about it already. Even Mr. Christenson, our history teacher, seemed surprised and impressed by what she said and the questions she asked."

Lena tried to write down as many things as possible that she remembered Grandmother had told her, especially about her return to Sweden in 1939, shortly before Hitler invaded Poland and everything seemed to crumble overnight. Even though history was not her best subject, Lena did like to study the war, for Grandmother had said things would have been different if it weren't for that madman, Hitler. Her unwillingness to talk about it much made Lena even more curious.

"Yes, Lena," said Sofia, "the Holocaust was a terrible time when many Jews, Gypsies, and political activists were murdered. I remember once when your grandmother broke down in sobs, regrets that her Jewish sister-in-law, Johann's wife, suffered so much from fear that her family in Poland might be taken to a concentration camp. It turned out that Johann did learn later that Rebecca's family was taken to Auschwitz-Birkenau, one of those camps you read about in your history class. They were all executed in the gas chambers. Johann wrote this news to your grandmother. It was just one more unpleasant memory for her."

Lena exclaimed, "Oh, how terrible—it must have been such a shock to learn that about Rebecca's family. Maybe it was good she never had to get that news—I mean Rebecca."

"Yes, I think you're right about that, Lena," Sofia said.

This information made Lena even more curious to learn more about Yael and her family. What had they suffered? She knew the family was Jewish because one Saturday when they were planning to get together, Yael said that she had to go to the synagogue for her Hebrew lessons first. Lena could empathize with Yael, remembering how Grandmother used to try to make her learn Swedish. She wondered if Yael had relatives who had died in the Holocaust.

Lena loved that Yael was far more gregarious and confident than her. She began to have more confidence in herself as Yael seemed to like the questions Lena asked in class. One day Yael invited Lena to come over to her house after school.

"Would you like to do our homework together? We could quiz each other to prepare for Mr. Christenson's test next week," Yael said.

Lena felt like her heart would leap right out of her chest. She was so happy to be invited to a friend's house, especially by someone she really admired, someone who always made smart comments in class and seemed to like the few she made, too. Lena knew Mr. Christianson appreciated the two girls for they were his best students—he told them so one day after a quiz.

As Yael and Lena walked to her house after school that day, they talked a lot about their families. Just as Yael was interested in learning about Lena's Swedish Grandmother, who she knew had committed suicide, Lena was interested in Yael's Jewish background, how it came to be she knew so much about Hitler and the Holocaust. Yael explained that her family had barely escaped the concentration camps, what she referred to as the "death camps." She said her parents, a young married couple at the time, finally managed to escape Germany in 1940, to flee to Portugal with many other Jews, where they were able to board the *SS Quanza*, a Portuguese passenger cargo ship bound for New York.

"It was a terrible and frightening time for my parents, Lena—for all Jews. My parents were among some of the luckiest. Actually, others escaped just in time from neutral countries, such as your grandmother's homeland, Sweden, before Hitler invaded Poland."

Lena was enthralled listening to her new friend with the big dark eyes, and hair as curly and black as Lena's was blonde and straight.

"Oh, please go on with your story, Yael," Lena said.

"Well, my parents were lucky to have relatives, some distant cousins in New York, who helped them. My father was smart and got a job as a bookkeeper at a garment factory. My mother said they wanted to have children right away, but she couldn't get pregnant. She said it was because of all the trauma she had suffered. That's why I came along much later. My mother was thirty-five years old when I was born."

"I remember my grandmother said something similar, that she lost her first child when she was only one month old. Her name was Lena, like mine. Grandmother said that it took her a long time to get pregnant again with my mother. But tell me more about your family, Yael."

"Well, my oldest brother, Mitch, was born in 1950, then came me in 1953, and my younger brother, Lenny, was born a year after. All us kids were born in New York, the city they call the Big Apple, but my mother longed to come to the West Coast where she had distant cousins in Portland. Last year, when I was fifteen, my father was offered work as a bookkeeper for a big shipping company in Astoria, and that's how we landed here, in this Scandinavian town of few Jews. Fortunately, we have a synagogue where we can meet other people like ourselves. It was hard starting high school, though, where I knew no one, in such a small isolated town—so small compared to New York. I'll be honest with you, Lena, I was miserable until I met you."

Astonished and delighted, Lena realized how much

the two of them had in common. Yael, though she seemed more confident, was as lonely as she was. Even though Lena had lived all her life in Astoria, she had never felt completely at home here, either. Yael and she had one more thing in common: they were both children of immigrants. Well, she admitted she was a second-generation child of a Swedish immigrant, while Yael was the child of first-generation immigrants. But that didn't make much difference. They could talk for hours about anything: literature, writing poetry, and their dreams to travel—even, sometimes, boys. Neither of them quite fit into the mold of mainstream America in small-town Astoria.

Lena told Yael how shy she felt around boys. "Maybe it's because I never had a father. My father was a fisherman, and he died when I was only a month old. I'm always so shy around boys and don't know what to say; besides, I tower over most of them. It's sometimes hard to be the tallest girl in the class."

"Yeah, Lena, I can understand that," said Yael. "I'm not exactly the shortest." The two girls laughed and linked arms as they walked down 12th Street towards Yael's house. "As far as boys go, for me, it's different. With two brothers teasing and hounding me all the time, I really don't pay too much attention to boys. I get enough of them at home. My older brother, Mitch, and I used to hang out together a lot in New York City, take the streetcar uptown after school and browse the shops and art galleries on Fifth Avenue."

Lena wondered what that would be like, to have siblings at all, let alone brothers. To live in a big city and browse galleries and department stores like those Yael described.

When the two girls arrived at Yael's house, she introduced Lena to her mother, who seemed much older than Sofia, but pleasant. She was about to go to the store and told Yael to have a nice time with her friend. She'd be back soon.

Yael invited Lena to see her bedroom and showed her a photo of her older brother. Mitch, she explained, was in college on the East Coast. She said she missed him. Lena thought he was terribly handsome. His dark piercing eyes and dark hair, so different from hers, attracted her. When she said that to Yael, she laughed. "Oh, Lena, I'm sure if he were here, he would like you, too. He always says he prefers blondes to brunettes."

"Really?" Lena looked surprised and blushed. She had never had anyone to talk to about boys and what they liked. Mother never encouraged her. And all Grandmother had ever said was "just you be careful around young men, Lena—don't let them get too friendly with you. You're too pretty a girl. You don't want to have what happened to your mother happen to you."

It was Yael who taught Lena the most about boys, their desires and what they liked in girls. She said she learned a lot from her brothers' conversations. Lena envied Yael's having brothers, but Yael explained it wasn't always "fabulous," that sometimes they could be pains, when they teased her or burst in on her when she was in the bathroom taking a bath and forgot to lock the door. Then there was the story about her boy cousin, who once tried to seduce her. Lena wasn't really quite sure what the word "seduce" meant but could guess. She had a vivid imagination. Another thing Lena loved about Yael was the way her breath smelled when she spoke, of freshly chewed spearmint gum—her favorite, she said. Grandmother had never allowed Lena to chew gum.

One day, Yael invited Lena to spend the night with her during their Christmas break and Mother finally agreed to it. Lena learned that the Jewish people didn't celebrate Christmas but instead had a religious holiday called Hanukkah. Yael showed her a beautiful brass candlestick she called a menorah; it had eight branches, and she said it was symbolic, that they used it when they celebrated Hanukkah. Lena began to feel that Yael was like a beloved sister, a sibling she never had. Maybe, she thought, this was how Grandmother felt about Rebecca. When she and Yael stayed overnight with one another, they would lie awake for hours, talking about so many things—their fantasies, their hopes and dreams for their futures. Like Lena, Yael dreamed of becoming a famous writer. They read Hemingway's *A Farewell to Arms* and *For Whom the Bell Tolls*. They'd lie on the grass outside Yael's house for hours in the summer and talk about the novels' love scenes, the conversations between the men and women characters. Some parts made Lena anxious, like the gruesome war scenes. Yael said they weren't so hard for her after overhearing her parents talk about relatives lost in concentration camps.

"Lena, war is part of life—as ugly as it is, it makes good stuff for novels," Yael said.

Lena felt that Yael was so much wiser than her.

It wasn't often that they talked about Lena's grandmother, about how she took her own life, leaving Mother and her in such an awful way, but on a particular day, as Lena's affection for Yael grew more and more strong,

Lena felt the need to share something, something deep inside herself, a longing, a memory. They had decided to walk to the beach, the small one down near the port, to do their homework together. Yael asked her if it was OK. At first, Lena didn't understand her question.

"Why, of course, I think that would be fun," Lena said.

"Are you sure, I mean, knowing, you know, well I mean ..." Yael seemed tongue-tied now, not knowing quite how to say something. Then she blurted out, "Well, I know your grandmother died near there, Lena. It was in the newspapers—don't you remember? My mother said the butcher at the Finnish meat market told her all about it. I know you must still miss her."

"Oh, yes, of course," Lena said. She didn't know quite what to say, at first. She guessed she had just buried so many details about her grandmother's death that she had momentarily blocked out the fact that Grandmother had died on the one and only small beach in Astoria.

"It's okay, Yael," she said. "My grandmother died— well, took her own life—almost two years ago. I had just turned fifteen at the time. I think I'm over the sadness of it now." Lena wanted to change the subject. "Let's go to the beach. It's such a sunny day; rare for here in March, isn't it?"

"Yes, good. That was my thought too, Lena," said Yael. "We can sit with our books in the sun for a change, maybe take our sweaters off and feel the warmth on our skin. Do you have any baby oil, by chance? We might be able to get a tan, a rare thing in Astoria."

"Oh, yes, that's a good idea, but I don't have any baby oil with me. Guess we'll just have to trust the sun."

As the two girls settled themselves down on their cardigan sweaters and organized their books, Lena's hand brushed Yael's. They looked up into each other's eyes and started giggling. Lena blurted out, "I almost feel like we're sisters." She turned away and felt the redness rise in her cheeks.

Yael laughed. "Yes, it's good for me, too. I can talk to you about things, Lena, I would never dare discuss with my brothers."

"That reminds me of something my grandmother once said to me. It was one of the very rare times she opened up with me. She told me about her brothers in Sweden and how she had always wanted a sister and then . . ." Lena hesitated.

"Please go on, Lena," Yael said, bending over her knees, which she had drawn up under her as she gazed in earnest at Lena with her big dark eyes.

"Well," Lena said, "I don't know a lot, but I think one reason my grandmother screamed at night is the loss she suffered of the one kind-of sister she had, her sister-in-law, wife of her older brother. Her name was Rebecca and, well, funny—I just remembered this. She was Jewish, too, like you, Yael."

"Oh, how interesting. How did she meet Rebecca? Here? When she immigrated to the United States?"

"Oh, no. You see, her brothers didn't immigrate with her; they stayed in Sweden, and her oldest brother met his wife, Rebecca, in Poland, I think, when he played the violin there—something like that. Grandmother met her sister-in-law the summer she returned to Sweden, in 1939. I think she was almost forty years old. She had my mother late in life, after losing her first baby."

"Oh, Lena, how sad," exclaimed Yael. "Yeah, my

mother always blames the trauma of the war and immigrating with great fear, for her miscarriages. My parents are older than a lot of my friends' parents. Sometimes it's hard since they seem a bit old fashioned and have so many ideas from the old country. Thank goodness for my brothers. Sorry to interrupt you—please go on about Rebecca."

"Well, my mother says that my grandmother wanted to return to Sweden to show her off. She was five years old at the time. My great grandparents had died already during the Spanish flu pandemic in 1919, five years after my grandmother immigrated. When Grandmother decided to return to Sweden, it was 1939, you know, just before Hitler invaded Poland and the horrors of the Holocaust took place.

Yael's eyes welled up with tears. "Oh, believe me, I know all about that. My brothers and I have grown up hearing our parents' stories of relatives we lost. But go on about your grandmother and this woman named Rebecca."

"All I know, Yael, is Grandmother said she felt very close to her sister-in-law, even though she hadn't known her long when she suddenly died, mysteriously. That's all Grandmother would say. When I'd ask her to explain more, she'd get impatient and upset, and end the conversation. I think my grandmother had many secrets she took with her when she walked into the ocean."

Lena turned aside, embarrassed, as she was the one tearing up now.

"Well," Yael said, "I guess that means they didn't know how she died—maybe she was killed by someone who hated Jews. I wasn't going to tell you this, Lena, but I remember my father once said that Hermann Göring, a Nazi and Commander-in-Chief of the German Air Force, was well-liked by a Swedish count of some repute, a pro-Nazi. Göring even built a house for the Swedish woman he loved—I think in southern Sweden where your relatives are from."

Lena's mouth dropped open in shock. "Oh, Yael, Grandmother never mentioned that to me. Mr. Christensen said Sweden was neutral during WWII—but are you suggesting there were unknown ties between Germany and Sweden?"

"All I'm saying, Lena, is that not all Swedish and Germans were enemies. Maybe someone who didn't like Jews in Sweden killed your grandmother's sister-in-law."

For a moment Lena sat in shock with this revelation. Maybe Yael was correct—and maybe that was why Grandmother hadn't wanted to talk about Rebecca. Lena vowed that someday she would learn the truth. For now, she kept this information to herself and never shared it, even with her mother.

Yael fidgeted with the buttons on her sweater and said, "Well, I've probably said too much, Lena. I don't want you to suffer any more about your grandmother's screams. Come on, let's study for our history test, shall we?" Yael looked down at her papers, and then reached over, not saying a thing, and handed Lena a Kleenex. Lena knew she and Yael understood each other's feelings and didn't need to say more.

But Lena did say, "Thank you, Yael, guess that's what sisters are for." They looked at each other, then threw their arms around each other and pulled away, giggling. Lena took a deep breath and thought, that must be what it's like to have a sister—that must be how Grandmother Helga felt, at least until Rebecca died. She hoped down deep she wouldn't lose Yael.

Two months later, at the end of the school year, Yael announced that her family had to move back to New York to be nearer relatives and a better job for her father. It would be many years later before Lena would meet up with Yael again. They wrote letters to one another, but they grew further and further apart as their lives took different paths.

Chapter 11

Later after Yael moved away and Lena was in her first year at Clatsop Community College she sometimes worried about her mother working so hard, spending her days making clothes for other women, fitting her patrons, putting up their hems and listening to their stories of dances, weddings , and other events that Sofia never had the opportunity to attend, working so hard at her sewing business. Lena tried to summon memories of her mother during happier times. She recalled a day when she came home early from her college classes. Sofia was usually either with customers or sewing alone in the double-doored dining room that she'd converted to her office and sewing room. Lena often heard her familiar humming.

On this particular day, Lena remembered her mother calling out to her, "You can come in, Lena. Mrs. Olsen and her daughter just left."

Lena set down her bookbag in the hall, removed her heavy, wet, yellow slicker raincoat and hung it on the hook above the wood-framed antique mirror, pulled off her muddy galoshes, and walked into Mother's sewing room.

"Ye gods, it was pouring like mad out there!" Lena said. "I was nearly soaked to the bone." Lena headed towards the floral-chintz-covered armchair in the room, one of her favorites, plopped down on it, and tucked her bell-bottom-covered legs under her. Pumpkin came around the corner of the open door, slunk towards her, and jumped into her lap, his favorite place to curl up. He always knew when she came home from school. Lena petted him as Mother looked up and slid a thimble off her index finger, holding on to her fine needle and the white taffeta on her lap.

"You're home early. Was there trouble at school again, more student sit-ins?"

"I don't know exactly," Lena said. "They just announced that all afternoon classes were cancelled: Something about a student strike. I left campus, glad to get home so I could work on my new story for my English class. Frankly, those poli-sci students who are always protesting about something bore me and I'm glad not to be a part of their rowdiness. They're too obstreperous for me."

Sofia raised an eyebrow. "My, aren't you starting to use big words."

It was 1970, the Vietnam war was raging, and Lena was going through some big changes, including with her wardrobe. She was too shy to wear those short skirts they called miniskirts, but she did love bell-bottom pants and wooden bead necklaces. She no longer wore braids, either, but preferred her hair in a long ponytail.

Her mother just looked at her as she ran out the

door in the mornings and laughed. "It's sure good your Grandmother Helga isn't here to see you. She'd have kittens."

Sofia looked up now from her sewing and started to talk where they had left off about the student sit-ins: "Well, dear, it's good you avoid those student riots. I'd hate to see you get involved and hauled off to jail."

Lena wanted to change the subject and glanced around the room to see what projects mother had going—a new wedding dress on her dress form, one draped over her chair, and the one in her hand. She couldn't help but comment, "I see you're working so hard, Mother. I worry about you never having enough time for yourself to have fun."

Sofia hummed softly as she bent over, boning a bodice on a new wedding dress; she had taught Lena some sewing terms, and Lena liked this one. It might, Lena thought, make a good phrase in one of her poems or stories. "Boning a bodice"—how interesting. Anyway, when Lena said this, Sofia looked up, her tired eyes ringed by dark circles, and smiled at Lena.

"Lena, don't worry. I love what I do." She looked down again at her hands and said, "These hands work hard—yes, it's true—but they make so many other women happy that when I see one of ours, a Swedish woman whose beautiful daughter is about to be married, like Mrs. Gustafsson's, I feel great pleasure. In fact, I've just finished her mother-of-the-bride dress, and I'm almost done with her daughter's wedding gown. Do you want to see it?" She held out the lacy bodice she had been working on and reached for the bottom half in white taffeta.

"What do you think?"

"Oh," Lena exclaimed, "it's lovely, Mother." In the back of her mind, Lena wondered if she would ever wear a wedding dress, but doubted it. She hadn't yet had her first date.

Sofia went on, "Mrs. Gustafsson and her daughter were just here. When they left, they turned as they were about to exit and said '*Tack så mycket*, we love our dresses, Sofia.' That was enough to make my day, besides the nice big deposit they gave me. I'll get the rest in a couple of days." Sofia went back to her bodice and seemed lost in a kind of dream world, then looked up at Lena. "Lena, I hope one day I will make a wedding dress for you."

In a whisper, Lena said, "Fat chance."

Lena liked boys, at least she thought she did—the smart ones. Most of them seemed childish and boring. She wanted an exciting life, and if it was ever going to be with a boy, he would have to have the same desire for adventures beyond Astoria that she had. Besides, it wasn't an issue now—most of them didn't look at her with any interest.

Sofia rose from her sewing machine and walked over to Lena to put her hands on her shoulders. "I know, dear, you worry that you're not dating like other girls at school. But don't worry. Someday the right young man will come along, see your beauty and your intelligence."

Almost disgusted, Lena said, "Don't worry, Mother. So far, no boys seem interested in me. And besides, I'm not sure I ever want to marry. I want to be a writer and live in Paris, in a turreted apartment, and spend my days at my typewriter and walk along the Seine reciting poetry."

Sofia laughed. "Oh, Lena, you're a romantic. That French teacher of yours is certainly getting under your skin. Your Grandmother Helga warned me about your romantic nature and always said I should curb your appetite for fantasy. Besides, you're wrong about no boy ever being interested in you. Last week, when I waved good-bye to you as you set off for your classes, I saw Lars Erikson watching you from the corner. I think he's shy, but really hopes to attract your attention."

Lena admitted to herself that she had seen Lars looking over at her during church services. He was good-looking, but no Darcy or Rhett Butler, the two men she most fantasized about from reading Austen's and Mitchell's novels in high school.

"Lena, I lost you," said Sofia. "You look like you're going off into one of your daydreams."

"Oh, I'm sorry, Mother. I was just wondering if I could compare Lars with any of the handsome characters that I love in the novels I read." Lena longed for her mother to see her, not just as her daughter but as a woman, like her, but different too, with the same kinds of longings Lena was pretty sure Sofia must have had— at least when she'd been Lena's age. Hadn't that been the age she'd fallen in love with Lena's father?

Sofia went on: "Lena, you just scare the young men with your beauty and your intelligence. They wither away, not knowing how to approach you. You have Helga's beauty. Why do you think her best friends always called her Goldie? It was because of her golden-colored hair, which you inherited. She wasn't always as you knew her, dowdy and with greying hair . . ." Sofia's voice trailed off, as if she were remembering Grandmother. "Lena, you have much of your grandmother in you—her determination and her stoicism."

Lena couldn't help but think to herself that it was her mother who had all the stoicism.

After a pause, Mother went on: "Well, I better clean up now. Why don't you go and freshen up, and tonight we'll go out to a restaurant for dinner. Mrs. Olsen paid me well today and we can celebrate a bit."

Lena's mouth dropped open at that suggestion. She and Mother rarely went out to eat or went anywhere together that was fun—grocery shopping or to the five-and-dime maybe but nowhere else, not even to the library. Lena usually hung out there alone, which she didn't mind. She loved getting lost in the stacks.

Lena whispered under her breath, "It's a good thing Grandmother Helga can't hear about our going out to dinner." Lena knew that Helga had been frugal, never one for extravagance. She'd thought her Swedish cooking was so good that nothing else could match it.

"Oh, Mother," Lena said, "yes, let's. How about the Italian restaurant? I love spaghetti and meatballs—they're different from Grandmother's."

"You're right, they are," said Sofia. "That's a good idea. Grab your coat and I'll get mine and we'll go to Bartoli's."

Chapter 11

As Lena continued her research in preparation for her entry into the Rotary Club and Clatsop College writing contest, she tried to recall more details about her grandmother to include in her story. "The telling is in the details," Mrs. Olsen had said.

When Grandmother was alive, Lena was always alert to clues as to why she screamed at night and to what may have occurred during her visit to Sweden. She recalled one particular day when she and her mother sat at the kitchen table drinking coffee (she laughed remembering how Grandmother always said, "You aren't a good Swede, Lena, unless you drink coffee.") On that day she remembered Grandmother walked into the kitchen holding a letter postmarked from Sweden that had just arrived. Lena loved the pretty stamps on the blue tri-folded lightweight air-mail stationery. As her grandmother began to read the letter, Lena was all ears.

In the letter, Johann discussed a lot about "Axel's progress," how he was maturing and doing well.

"Who's Axel?" Lena blurted out. Grandmother cast

an evil eye at her as she looked up from the letter.

"He's the little boy you saw in the photo handing flowers to your mother when we visited Sweden, you know, in that photo I showed you. Well, he's not really a boy now, though he was six or seven when that photo was taken. He's two years older than your mother. He was born not quite right in the head and, in some ways, I guess, remains like a young boy. He's not Johann's real son, you know." Grandmother looked down at her lap and fidgeted with the letter in her hands. "His father—well, his father was Gunnar, who died. Johann adopted him and raised him all these years."

Sofia looked over the edge of her coffee cup at Lena as she sipped her coffee, as if to say, be careful Lena, don't ask too many questions.

Lena's curiosity got the best of her and she said, "Oh, how did Gunnar die, Grandmother?"

Aggravated, Grandmother peered at her over the letter and said, "Lena, I've told you over and over not to ask so many questions. I don't know how he died." She stuffed the letter into her apron pocket and pushed back her chair. Its legs made a scraping sound on the already-scratched kitchen floor. Then she stood up, turned, and walked out of the room. Sofia just went on humming softly under her breath.

That wasn't the first time Grandmother shared a letter from Johann. In another one, he told of how much he missed Rebecca. He said he regretted he had not been able to find her sister, Suzanna, who had been sent to Denmark by her parents in Poland to escape being picked up by the Nazi soldiers. Grandmother stopped reading Johann's letter to explain that when the Nazis invaded Denmark, many of the children were sent to Sweden and eventually were adopted by Swedish families. She knew Johann had hoped to find Suzanna.

Lena made a note of this interesting information. She thought to herself, she'd have to do some research at their local library. She knew the librarian liked her and understood her interest in her grandmother's past. She would be helpful.

On another occasion, when Grandmother was in a better mood and sharing some photos from her album with Lena, she made an oblique reference to Nazis. As Helga turned the pages of the album, Lena noticed a photo missing by the empty space it left. It was a page of photos of Helga's brothers, when they were young, maybe eighteen and twenty, just before Grandmother immigrated to America.

"Why is there a missing photograph, Grandmother?"

Grandmother became irritated, slammed the album shut like a clamshell, and said, "Oh, Lena, you would not have liked to know him, my brother Gunnar. He was bad, got mixed up with the wrong people before the war. I cannot tell you more." Then she stomped off towards her bedroom and slammed the door.

Chapter 12

Every moment Lena had free from her chores, her part-time weekend job at JC Penney, and her homework, she wrote. She'd come home from school, grab her journal, and go to her secret spot under the back porch. Having reached her full height now of five feet, eight inches, she could no longer easily fit there and had to sit with her legs outstretched. Her mother would laugh when she came out to see Lena's legs poking out from under the porch while she hung the laundry or picked a few veggies from their garden plot. She had known about Lena's so-called secret spot for a long time but had never made fun of her until now.

"Lena, don't you think you should find another place to write? She laughed and said: "You don't have to worry now about Grandmother harassing you and I certainly won't—I'm too busy with my sewing orders. I'll respect wherever you would like to write, dear, and not bother you."

The Astorian fog started to roll in. Lena was chilled to the bone. Mother was right. Reluctantly Lena tore down the last vestiges of her secret space. The old orange crate where she had kept her favorite books and the worn mohair cushion went into the garbage. From then on, she wrote in her room until the wee hours of the night. She was almost finished with her story.

At dinner one night, Mother asked, "Well, Lena, how's the writing going? Are you still working on that story for the college writing contest?"

"Yes, but I'm struggling with the ending," said Lena. "With Mrs. Olsen's encouragement, I'm taking one small slice of Grandmother's life, her trip to Sweden in 1939, before WWII, and fictionalizing it, of course. The hardest part for me is talking about the mysterious trauma she must have suffered there—how do I write about something I don't know—something that must have happened during her 1939 visit with you, Mother, that was horrible enough to make her take her own life."

"Since we don't know what really happened there, Lena, the ending should be easy." said Mother. "You can end it in about any way you want. Make up something. You've got an imagination."

"Yes, you're right, I guess," said Lena. "My professor said he'd call it 'An Immigrant's Story,' a story that is common all over the world—of course, many immigrants' lives hang in the balance; they often don't know where they'll end up, do they? Maybe I can weave that into the story." Lena tapped her head lightly with her pencil.

Mother smiled. "No, my clever daughter, I guess they don't. You'll find the right ending and title for your story, I'm sure of that. Now, let's set the table. I'm hungry, aren't you? Grandmother's soup's almost ready.

You can put the bread out, too."

• • •

By the following year, Lena had finished the story, leaving the ending for the reader to decide. Mrs. Olsen, her former high school English teacher, had met with her several times during the summer and liked the story. Lena entered the contest, and a month after that, she received the good news that she had won the scholarship. She would be spending her next academic year in Paris, France. She came home elated to give her mother the good news. She nearly stumbled up their wooden front stairs as she ran towards the screen door, pulled it open, and shouted out, "I won, I won."

Mother, bent over her sewing in the parlor, looked up dazed a minute until she grasped the full meaning of what Lena was saying. "Lena, I'm so proud of you. You know your grandmother would have been too, even though she sometimes seemed to want to discourage your writing career. Down deep, I think that she admired you and your perseverance. It wasn't that different than hers. You are just luckier to live in a different time."

"Maybe that's true, Mother," said Lena. "But all I know now is that I feel like a big red balloon has just lifted me up, like the one in my favorite childhood story, the one you read to me, *The Red Balloon*, and I'm about to fly away to a new life in Paris."

• • •

When Lena wasn't writing or working, she was day-dreaming about the next year in Paris. She continued to write short stories, which she entered in state and local contests. She even received a small stipend from one Oregon journal of women's literature, for her short story about a young Finnish girl who arrives alone and frightened in a fishing town near Willapa Bay, Washington. Of course, all of it was from her imagination but inspired by her grandmother's life. The timing of her stories was propitious. It was the 1970s, and there was mounting concern about immigrants taking American jobs during a time of economic and political uncertainty. Lena tried to paint a realistic view of the challenges that immigrants, like her grandmother and grandfather, had faced in earlier times. In spite of the backlash and prejudice against immigrants, farmers and factories were clamoring for their cheap labor. Lena included these facts in her fictional story.

Lena's views weren't always well-accepted when she was in school, but she was developing more self-confidence now that she knew she would be leaving small-town Astoria and starting a new life in Paris, France. She had no idea what lay ahead. The closer she got to her departure date, the more nervous she felt, and the less she slept.

"Mother," she said one day, "it's like a whole hive of bees are buzzing about in my brain. I can't sleep at night thinking about what's ahead for me."

"Why don't you try making lists, Lena, of what you want to take with you and where you hope to go once in Paris, places you might want to visit. Maybe you'll be able to sleep better once you have written down some of the things buzzing about in your brain."

"I'm worried my writer's brain will just shut down and freeze, that once at the Sorbonne, I won't be able to write a poem, or even live up to Mrs. Olsen's expectations and be able to complete the year."

Sofia laughed. "Oh, Lena, don't worry, you've proved you can do it and you will be a great success, I'm sure, but only if you get adequate sleep."

Sofia had worried about Lena's problems sleeping for a long time. She had even taken her to a doctor when she was a freshman in high school and a teacher complained that Lena sometimes "drifted off" while he was lecturing. Sofia blamed the nights she knew her daughter's sleep had been interrupted by Helga's nightmares, but there was nothing she could do about that. The doctor prescribed a mild sleeping pill, but it didn't seem to help that much. In a way, she understood. She had similar problems as a child, awakened so many times by her mother's screams.

One of Lena's worries was about how her mother would manage being alone without her help with grocery shopping, housecleaning, and meal preparation, while keeping up her sewing business. Would her mother get lonely? She certainly didn't have a big social life. Mostly it was just going to church choir practice and occasionally getting together with their neighbor, much older than herself, for tea. She wished Mother would realize that she was still attractive—she had seen handsome Mr. Grimly, the shoe-store owner, a Norwegian, look at Mother when they went to buy Lena new shoes for her trip.

At least she and Mother had a plan to go to Sweden when she finished her studies. She hoped that dream would help bolster her mother during her long days working at her sewing.

The big day of Lena's departure finally came. She was euphoric as she and Mother waited on the front porch, beside Lena's one big suitcase and her backpack. She bit her nails and nearly wet her pants as they saw their friend, Sven, drive up in front of the house. An old fishing friend of her father's, he had volunteered to take them to the Portland Airport for Lena's departure. He had "things to pick up in town," he said. "It wouldn't be an inconvenience." Lena secretly thought Sven was sweet on Sofia, but she knew her mother didn't give him any encouragement.

Three hours later, after a bumpy ride over the mountains, Lena and her mother had a tearful good-bye. Mother's last words were, "Remember, Lena, we'll go to Sweden to find out more about Grandmother's past as soon as you finish your studies next spring."

Part II

Lena in Paris 1973

Chapter 13

The first few weeks in Paris were a blur: getting settled in my small room at the student residence, an old nineteenth century multistoried building with a mansard roof; meeting my new friend, Michelle; attending my first classes in French and then discovering the art studio where I went to draw a few times, the place where I met Joseph.

I had a sketch book and drawing pencils Mother had given me just before my departure for Paris. I loved sketching the new scenes I encountered every day, when crossing the Luxembourg Gardens after classes at the Sorbonne: children sailing toy boats in the big round pond or the stone baroque sculptures of famous people out of French history, which hid themselves in various parts of the lushly treed park. It was all fascinating to me. I loved studying people in the cafes where I went for coffee after class: the old Frenchmen with their *Paris Match* magazines; the fashionable women in their high heels and big patent tote bags, leaning in over round tables as they greeted friends, seeming to share their deepest, darkest secrets; the waiter who rushed by with trays of coffee or Perrier, baguettes, or fluffy whipped-cream-topped desserts. I soaked it all up—Paris was mine.

One day, Michelle told me about an art studio, an *atelier*, where I could go and draw from models. Her boyfriend was an artist. "There's a great little street you will want to explore, la Rue de la Grande Chaumière, just off Boulevard Montparnasse," she said. "There, you'll find the best art studio in Paris and there is a good art supply shop on the same street. Artists like Modigliani, Picasso, and Gauguin used to go and sketch there. It's not expensive. "You'll have to check out the times the models pose."

"*Vraiment?*" I questioned her with excitement. My heart skipped a beat. "Oh, Michelle, it sounds wonderful. But I don't have a lot of time between my classes and studies. Is it far away?"

"No, not at all, by metro. I'll draw you a map after we leave Professor Michaud's class," said Michelle. Michaud was our French poetry prof—stern, but I liked him and adored learning more about the poetry of the modernists like Charles Baudelaire and Paul Verlaine, whose poem I would recite as I went to sleep at night:

"*Il pleure dans mon couer comme il pleut sur la ville...*"

That was the first poem that attracted me to French poetry. The words of the rain as a metaphor for someone's tears sang through my mind. It said what I often felt: "It cries in my heart like it rains on the city." It reminded me in some ways of the way I had felt when Grandmother died, so many years ago now. How long ago was it? Five years?

I was thrilled to have met Michelle, really my first friend since Yael had moved away from Astoria. Sometimes I had the impression, though, that she was so much more sophisticated than I would ever be, with confidence I hoped I would eventually possess.

Each day in Paris I felt more at home and enraptured by this new city they called City of Lights and its culture! The day I decided to go to the art studio was a bit overcast. Classes had been cancelled for All Saints Day. It was autumn and the leaves on the giant chestnut trees along the paths of the Tuileries Gardens where I loved to stroll were changing color to yellow and soft rust. I decided it was high time I went to the studio that Michelle had suggested.

I loved taking the Metro, the underground train system, except during rush hour. It was like an artist's drawing of a maze of swirling, twisting black lines on white paper all heading in different directions, underground and sometimes over. I pushed past the crowds in the underground tunnel as I found my departure platform; my train pulled in and throngs of people got off. I pushed past them and boarded just in time, as the doors slammed shut. Three stops later, I ascended the long steep stairs out of the metro station as other passengers brushed past me. It was good to come up onto the street level and breathe the brisk autumn air. I pulled out the pocket-sized map Michelle had given me and looked for the two spots she had marked, showing me the way to the studio. There it was, the short and narrow street, Rue de la Grande Chaumière, just off Boulevard Montparnasse.

She had said to look for the short alley-like street, and then halfway down, on the right side, the sign that said Atelier de la Grande Chaumière. "Just ring the bell and they'll let you in." It seemed so simple, but my old nervousness about anything new kicked in. Should I come back on another day? I fingered my worn Metro map in my pocket and decided it was now or never.

Just then a male voice from behind me said, "Mademoiselle, may I help you? You look lost."

I nearly jumped out of my skin before I could turn around and look up at him to reply. "Oh, no, I'm fine, just looking for the art studio—the one where people can draw from models."

As he came closer and faced me, I could see the man was medium height, slightly shorter than I was, handsome, and maybe five or six years older. He was carrying a big portfolio under his arm. He smiled. "I'm going there now. Would you like me to accompany you?"

My usual shyness around men bubbled up to the surface, and I said, "Oh, merci, but no. I have some errands to do," which, in a way, was true. I wanted to stop at the art supply shop that Michelle had told me was near the studio.

"As you wish, mademoiselle." He nodded his head. His long black hair dropped casually across his left eye, and he went on. I saw him enter the building nearer the end of the street on the opposite side from where I stood.

I sucked in my breath with relief but couldn't help wondering if I had passed up a good chance to meet a possible future boyfriend. I continued to walk up the narrow street and came to the art supply shop. I peered into the window at the enthralling display of art materials: pinewood paint boxes with lids open to display tiny tubes of oil paints, piles of brushes of all sizes and shapes, containers of pastel chalks, colors like ice cream flavors. There was a sign on the door: *Fermé*. I hoped the shop would be open when I finished at the studio. Luckily, I had a sketchbook, a few pieces of charcoal, and some drawing pencils with me.

A bit nervous, I hesitated for a moment at the big black door of the atelier, then pressed the buzzer to its right. A large imposing man with slightly longish, oily, stringy hair under a black beret, dressed in a voluminous dark blue artist's smock, greeted me.

"Well, bonjour, Mademoiselle. Are you coming for our life drawing session?"

"Oui, Monsieur," I said.

"I suppose you have your own drawing pad and materials with you?"

I nodded my head and said, "They're right here in my backpack." I removed and opened it to show him. "Will these do?"

"Oui," said the man, who I later learned went by the name Monsieur Louie. "Your drawing pad is a bit small. You may want to purchase a larger one up the street at the art supply store, but for now it's best to see if you like this experience. The model will pose in that room down the hall and to your left, in ten minutes." He pointed out the direction to me. "I suggest you find a spot to sit. That will be ten francs, please."

I slipped my coin purse out of my pocket and handed the money to Monsieur Louie.

"Now, *depechez-vous*, hurry and find a seat, Mademoiselle."

I walked down the darkish hallway and opened another black door to push through a thick maroon velvet curtain. The light in the room was dim, and it took a moment for my eyes to adjust. I looked across the room, which was round. In the center stood a raised platform next to a large potbelly stove putting out some heat, for which I was glad on this rather cool night. There was a stool on the platform. The seating for those coming to draw was a semi-circle of raised steps going up five levels surrounding the center stage. I headed for a seat about three levels up on the right side, sat down, and pulled out my sketchbook, drawing pencils, and some charcoal sticks from my backpack. As I opened to the first page of the sketchpad, a woman wrapped in a burgundy-colored satiny silk robe walked in with long languid steps and took her place on the stage. Her feet were bare. She pulled her auburn-colored hair up into a knot on top of her head, removed her robe. I beheld a beautiful female nude. I was not shocked, as I had once taken a life-drawing class at the Clatsop Community College. My worse moments had been when I'd first looked at male models. Having grown up without a father, amongst only women, I was shy and inhibited around men. To gaze at a man in the nude was, at first, intimidating. But by the end of the term, I was quite adjusted and sometimes had to admit that I found the male models the most fun to draw, with their defined muscles and interesting angular faces.

I made a furtive glance around the room while the model prepared her pose. As my eyes adjusted to the dim light, I realized there were only nine people there, mostly men, and one other woman. The man I had met in the street sat directly across from me. Our eyes met for a split second; he smiled, I looked down. I pulled my attention back to the model, then to my drawing pad, and began to sketch. I was mesmerized by the model's poses, some when she seemed to twist in half, her upper torso, with its small firm breasts, turned one way and her lower body the other direction, her long legs slightly apart. After a few standing poses, she sat and even kneeled, giving the artists a chance to observe her beautiful frame in every imaginable pose. Some were only five or ten minutes, and then she took a few longer ones. Time passed quickly. I seemed to drop all my cares and thought little of anything else but that which was in front of me.

While I drew, I sensed the man across the room watching me. I was afraid to take my eyes off the model or my drawing pad. Finally, I could not resist. It was like a magnetic pull. I looked up and my eyes connected with those of the dark-haired man. His intense eyes were fixed on me. His gaze made me nervous, and I returned my eyes to my drawing. Later, while the model took a short break, I stood up to go and get a drink of water. I had spied a water cooler in the corner of the room. I was aware that the man across the room continued to watch me, even as he seemed to be organizing his drawing materials for the last half hour of the session. The time flew by, and soon Monsieur Louis entered, walked over to the model, handed her an envelope, which she discreetly slipped into the pocket of her robe before she exited the room with a brisk step.

"*C'est ca*! That's it," announced Monsieur Louis to the people around the room as they began to don their coats and scarves, slip their sketches into portfolios and an assortment of carrying devices. Some chatted with one another, others just mumbled to themselves as they examined their drawings before placing them in their portfolios. I returned my sketchpad to my backpack and put my pencils away in the small canvas carrier my mother had given me, all the while aware of the eyes across the room, still focused on me. As I was exiting the velvet curtain, I felt a gentle grip on my arm. Surprised, I pulled my arm away and looked up into those same dark eyes that had met mine earlier from across the room.

With an expression of confidence, the man said, "Excusez-moi, Mademoiselle, my name is Joseph. I'm sorry if I seemed to be staring at you. I hope you aren't offended. I couldn't help but notice the intensity with which you studied and drew, as if trying to capture every curve of the model's body in one stroke of charcoal. Your concentration was impressive. I often work with artists. Would you care to join me for coffee, *s'il vous plait*?" The stranger spoke English with a charming French accent.

I was awash in shyness and didn't know exactly how to reply to the forwardness of this Frenchman, if I should be afraid or flattered. "Uh, well, I'm not sure I can do that," I said haltingly. "I have to catch the metro and get back to my residence before it gets any darker."

"I understand," he said. "May I accompany you? We could talk on the way."

"No, thank you. I plan on stopping at the art store to buy some supplies and would prefer to go alone," I said finally.

The man persisted, "Well, by chance, if you're coming again to the studio—I come every Wednesday—I hope you'll accept my invitation in the future. I'll be glad to accompany you safely back to your residence. Please accept my card."

The man handed me a card on which I read the

name, Joseph Hoffman, Galerie Bleu. Could it be that he was an art-gallery owner? Flustered, I said, "Merci. I must go now." I proceeded to walk to the exit. "Au revoir."

Outside, the air was crisp and chilly. I breathed a sigh of relief and headed quickly down the street, all the while wondering if I would dare accept this man's invitation in the future, if he was serious. His dark piercing eyes and full-lipped smile attracted me. I was curious to know more about him. As I passed the art supply shop, I noticed the sign in the window still said Fermé (closed). Disappointed, I continued walking in the direction of the metro entrance, pondering when I would next be able to come to the studio—next Wednesday, perhaps? Maybe I would have to skip one of my classes.

Once on the metro, I watched the many people getting on and off, coming from work, all sorts of people, some with dark skin, some with foreign-looking clothing, Arabs, Africans, sophisticated Frenchmen with scarves wrapped around their throats, holding their briefcases close to their bodies. People jostled to get on and off the underground train before it started moving again. The man named Joseph slipped quickly from my mind. I probably would never see him again, anyway, I concluded.

Chapter 14

As busy as I was attending classes, keeping up with my homework, and trying to write a message to Mother from time to time on one of the thin blue aerograms—she had packed many in my suitcase, a gentle reminder to write—I had little time for a social life or to make new friends. Michelle was often occupied with her boyfriend. We'd get together for coffee at a café near the Sorbonne from time to time, but that was all. One day at one of our coffee dates, I shared the difficulty I was having on an assignment from Professor Michaud. Not being completely fluent in French, I sometimes missed certain subtleties in Verlaine's poems.

Michelle suggested I look for an English version. She knew just the place, a Paris icon for writers in English, the Shakespeare and Company bookstore on the Left Bank, not far from the Île de la Cité. I took her suggestion and headed there right after our coffee date.

It was a bitterly cold day, not damp like Astoria, but with the same grey skies and chilly air. After ascending the metro, I shivered and pulled my heavy neck scarf, the one Grandmother had knit with the Scandinavian motifs, closer around my throat. I was wearing one of her knit caps as well. My hands wished I had remembered my mittens. I finally arrived at the bookstore and walked in, happy to get out of the cold. Immediately, I was drawn into its depths. The store had a musty smell, that of old books and paper. Here and there were beds tucked in amongst the shelves where writers-in-residence were occasionally allowed to spend nights while they did research in exchange for helping around the store. What a novel idea, I thought, as I began to look for the section on French poets. It didn't take me long. I began to pull out a few of the smallish, faded-red-covered books with the antique-styled type on the front. As I perused the yellowed pages of the books, I could almost hear the dry music of the writer's pen composing the poems. I was just about to pull out another of the books, a heavier one, when my elbow touched that of another, a boy—no, a man, who stood next to me and reached for the same book.

"Oh, excusez-moi," he said, in a thick accent, not French, which I always recognized. "Not a lot of space is there, between the aisles?"

I just stood there, frozen in shyness for a moment.

"Were you by chance looking for this book?" the stranger continued as he pulled it from the shelf. "Here." He placed it in my hands. "I don't need it."

Finally, I found my tongue, "Oh, no—I mean, yes. Thank you, merci!"

The stranger had robin's-egg-blue eyes like mine, and I could see sandy-colored hair peeking out from under his black wool cap. Our eyes locked for a moment. He smiled, turned, and continued down to the end of the aisle and was out of sight. I wondered about his accent. His English was good, but there was an accent. Yes, it was like Grandmother's—of course. I put him out of my mind, or tried, and pulled two more books out of the stacks, one on sonnets, the other on influences on Verlaine, which I could use for my assignment. I then walked back to the front of the store.

There, standing at the cash-register counter, was the stranger I had bumped elbows with. I paused to take him in, all about six feet of him. He was dressed in a leather jacket with a yellow woolen scarf around his neck. Yes, he was handsome. Something about him reminded me of someone. Perhaps it was a photo my mother had once given me—was it the blue eyes? No, it was the sandy-colored hair, the cap, almost a captain's style, and his square jaw. He looked like the photo Mother had given me to place in my locket, a gift from her on my sixteenth birthday. I couldn't get that image out of my mind as I set the books down at the end of the counter to get my coin purse out and reached up to feel my locket, which hung under my sweater—yes, that's it, I thought. He looks like my father, Eric Larsson.

He seemed to sense my staring at him, looked up, nodded at me, and said, "Hello, again." He waved his hands in front of my dazed eyes like a bird flapping his wings. "Are you still here?" He laughed.

"Oh, oui. I'm so sorry I was staring at you, but you remind me of someone," I said.

"Well, I hope he was nice and it's a good memory," said the blue-eyed stranger.

The storekeeper looked up and handed him the bag of books he had just purchased and his paper receipt. The stranger turned towards me again and said, "Well,

I'll be seeing you. *Adjö!*" He walked out.

Still dazed, I just waved. Adjö? That's it. Like a light bulb going on, I realized in a flash why he attracted my attention, besides the fact that he looked like my father. He's Swedish, I said to myself. I approached the check-out counter, paid for my books, and proceeded to leave the bookstore.

"Au revoir, Mademoiselle," said the storekeeper, an elderly man with longish grey hair and a beard, a friendly looking soul. Could he possibly be the famous owner, what was his name—Whitman—as in Walt? But his name was actually George. I remembered my French teacher had once told me about this famous bookstore owner in Paris.

"Au revoir," I said.

As I exited the store and started to walk towards the metro, I noticed the stranger again as he leaned against a lamppost where he seemed to be waiting for some-one—me perhaps.

He waved and asked, "May I walk with you? I think you may be Swedish and I'm new here in Paris. It would be great to have someone to speak Swedish with. My French isn't all that good."

My usual instincts to walk on and try to ignore the stranger were surpassed by my curiosity. "Sure, I'm headed for the metro."

"Me, too," he said. "Let me introduce myself. My name is Peter Lindstrom. What's yours, may I ask?"

"Lena. You're not right, though. I'm not Swedish ex-actly—well, partly so. My grandmother was a Swedish immigrant in America. I'm from the United States, studying here. Actually, I hope to go to Sweden one day and meet my relatives."

"Oh, great. I'm from Stockholm. Where was your grandmother from?" He glanced at the heavy bag I was carrying. "That bag looks heavy. May I carry it for you?"

"No, tack, I can put the books in my backpack." As I said this, I stopped to remove my backpack and place the bag of books in it. Peter reached to help me. Nice manners, I thought.

We walked on and discovered we were both students at the Sorbonne. By the time we got off of the metro, I was elated to realize I had made another friend, especially one from Sweden—he would understand perhaps something about what I had endured with a Swedish grandmother. Maybe Peter could help me with information about how to get to Sweden. Mother would be coming in the spring at the end of the school term to go there with me, or so I thought.

Chapter 15

I had no time to get to know Peter, nor Joseph, the man I'd met at the atelier. Two weeks after the incident at the bookstore, I received a telegram from Mrs. Lundberg saying my mother had fallen ill and I was needed at home to help care for her. She had been diagnosed with an aggressive cancer and was possibly not going to live long. As I read the note, I dropped to the floor in my room at my student residence, began to tremble all over, and let out a sob.

"Oh, no, Mother, you can't die—please, not now, not before I can make you proud of my success here in Paris, not before we can go to Sweden together."

But there was no one there to hear my pleas. The next two days went by in a fog as I made arrangements with the residence to keep my room, arranged my flight back to the US, and told my professors at the Sorbonne I had to leave but would be back—at least I hoped I would be. All the while I was devastated to think my mother was suffering. My new life in Paris was shattered by the news. I knew my mother needed me, and that was all that was important now. I cried myself to sleep for two nights, and the third day, red-eyed and exhausted, I boarded my flight at De Gaulle airport for my journey home.

Once back in Astoria, Oregon, I became immersed in my mother's care. For days, I sat in my grandmother's old rocking chair by my mother's bed while she slept. I had lots of time to reflect on her life and on Grandmother Helga's, too. I struggled to imagine my life without Mother. What would I do—how could I survive? My only solace was the feel of Pumpkin's soft fur as he sat in my lap and purred.

I remembered how I had learned to cope with Grandmother's frequent screams at night and her suicide. I tried to summon up the same strength again; sometimes, as a child, I would just fall asleep with a pillow over my head, but when I tried this now, I still could not get the thought of losing my mother out of my head. I was too distraught to even write in my journal, my other mode of dealing with things I couldn't face head on. I tried to remember only the good days, the Sundays we would make Swedish pancakes and douse them in lingonberry syrup. I fantasized how I would teach my new French girlfriend, Michelle, how to cook Swedish—if I ever got back to France.

I recalled how Mother once shared her remorse that I would never have a sister or brother, to give me support if something happened to her. Grandmother would pipe in, saying it was just as well—"three mouths are enough to feed." I could hear her words now: "Not enough money to stretch to feed another mouth around here, Sofia. Be glad you have Lena. She's a good girl and will be a big help to you when you get older."

Who would have thought that time would arrive so soon, Mother only thirty-nine and me, just twenty.

Lost in these thoughts, I was startled, on my second day back in Astoria, when Mother suddenly woke up, looked at me, and said, "Oh, dear Lena, I'm so sorry to have taken you away from your studies in Paris." She spoke in a whisper and looked pale and wan. "Tell me, please, more details about your first two months in Paris. How's that new girlfriend of yours—Michelle, is that her name? Do you like your professors? You mentioned in your aerograms the name of one—the poetry professor. Are you sleeping better?" The questions rolled off her tongue, one after another like the waves at the beach where we had spent so much time—happy and sad times.

"Mother, you must not tire yourself," I said, but then proceeded to tell her about Paris, to fill in the details I knew she would enjoy. I hesitated, then decided not to mention the man I met at the art studio, Joseph, though I found myself fantasizing that I would someday meet up with him again. But I did tell Mother about Peter. This appeared to delight her; she even found the energy to smile through her pain. The thought that I had met a Swedish boy, maybe her only dream.

I waited and after a few minutes she turned her head on the pillow towards me and said softly, "Your grandmother would be so pleased, Lena." She stroked my hand, which I laid at her side as I leaned in close to her. Eventually she drifted back to sleep with a smile on her face. There was no more humming from her or her sewing machine now, only faint breathing.

On the fourth morning after my return, I decided to try to make the Swedish pancakes Mother loved. Maybe they would help restore her energy. Make her feel better. I recalled how Grandmother would mix up a thin batter of flour, milk, and melted butter, then take out the heavy iron Swedish pancake griddle with the small round impressions where she'd pour the batter. I loved watching her grab a hairpin, one of those old-fashioned kind with the two wiggly sides, from her bun, and use it to flip up one side of each pancake as they bubbled. Grandmother explained that was how she could tell if they were ready to turn, when they were slightly golden in color. Once they were done on the other side, she'd flip them out of the griddle onto a plate and pour the fresh lingonberry syrup over them. They would melt in our mouths.

As I worked in the kitchen and hummed along with the pop music on our radio, I told myself the pancakes would be my surprise for Mother, bring back her energy somehow. They'd make her feel better, I hoped. Down deep I knew I was kidding myself, knew that mother was failing faster by the day. The doctor stopped by to visit every other day. All he said was she needed rest. He explained to me how to administer her medicines and how to keep her comfortable. I wondered if any of this was really helping.

I agonized over my mother's cancer. Why her? I remembered before I left for Paris, she sometimes doubled over in pain after a meal and a long day at her sewing machine. When I expressed worry, she'd smile and say, "Oh, of course, just tired. Too much sewing lately. I'll just take a break for a while. I'm sure I'll be fine." She was like that, always stoic.

Mrs. Lundberg stopped by to see Mother on occasion. Most of the time, Mother would just say a few words and then fall back to sleep. Sometimes Mrs. Lundberg would stay awhile and talk to me. On one of those days, she commented:

"It's good you came back from Paris, Lena. Your mother missed you very much. She worries about your difficulties sleeping and hopes it won't affect your studies in Paris. She wants the best for you. She lives with the hope that you will find out what keeps you awake at night and be able to use your talents for writing to have a better life than she has had."

At those words, I felt tears well up in my eyes. Brushing them aside, I said, "Mrs. Lundberg, thank you, but I want my mother to know I have had a good life." Under my breath I said, "I only wish she had." I went on to say "The one exception were the nights that Grandmother woke me with her nightmares and the sadness she brought to Mother and me when she committed suicide." I let my voice trail off.

Mrs. Lundberg patted me on the arm. "I know, Lena, but mothers want everything for their children, the best of everything. You will see someday when you have your own children."

To myself I thought—if I ever have my own.

As I stirred the pancake batter that morning after Mrs. Lundberg left, I thought back to the time when Grandmother left for a month to visit her friend Marta in Chicago. It was much quieter in our house for a while: no more sounds of her slippers shuffling down the hall, or the wooden spoon against the old crockery bowl when she stirred the cookie dough. Best of all, no more screams at night. I began to sleep better and my grades at school improved. That soon came to an end. Grandmother returned, as did the bad dreams, and I continued to struggle with sleeplessness.

Daydreaming while cooking the pancakes, I was startled when I heard Mother call out, "Lena, help me, please!"

I dropped the hairpin I was about to use to flip the pancakes, turned off the heat, and ran down the hall and up the stairs as fast as I could go, to find Mother on the floor. She had tried to get out of bed and had fallen. She was struggling to grab the bed frame to pull herself up.

"Wait, Mother, please—I'll help you," I said. "I have a surprise for you this morning for breakfast."

"Oh, dear, I'm afraid I don't have much of an appetite. Just take me to the bathroom and then let me sleep."

For the whole next week, the days passed slowly as I came to the realization my mother was rapidly slipping away. The doctor stopped by one more time. He was kind but couldn't hide what I knew was true—my mother was going to die. He just said in a soft voice with a hand on my shoulder, "Lena, you must prepare yourself."

Prepare myself? I screamed inside. How was I supposed to do that? That night I wept myself to sleep—sleep, the only solace I could find, and rarely did.

Our family certainly has had enough of death, I thought. With the loss of Grandfather in the war, Father out at sea, and Grandmother's suicide. It seemed to me this tragic thread of sadness and loss just went on and on. I glanced over at my mother whose breathing was coming hard now. I could not hold back the flood of tears. I'm glad Mother never awoke to see them.

A day later, my mother, Sofia Johansson-Larsson,

passed away. I was devastated. Mrs. Lundberg stayed at the house with me for several nights. The Swedish community took up a collection for Mother's cremation. Now I would have the ashes of the two most important people in my life to scatter on some hallowed ground in Sweden—if I ever made it there. The funeral service was in the Lutheran Church on the other side of town up on the hill. All the fishing community was there. The ladies from the Swedish Salvation Army prepared food.

After the service, the community had a kind of party, but not a happy one, in the church reception hall. I could barely stand up for it, but Mrs. Lundberg said, now that I was the head of the family—I screamed inside, "What family?"—I would have to try to greet everyone. Finally, the last person drifted out of the church social hall.

Out of nowhere came Lars Erickson, an old classmate. He approached me with some empathy in his eyes and said, "Hello, Lena. I'm sure sorry for your loss. Do you remember me?"

My mind raced back to my high school days and the times I looked over to find Lars staring at me.

"Oh, yes, I do, Lars. How are you?"

"I'm fine. I'd like to take you home, if you need a ride."

Just then, Mrs. Lundberg approached. She seemed to know Lars and said, "Why hello, Lars, how are you?"

Lars appeared nervous and self-conscious as he stood on one foot and then the other. He was dressed in a nice blue shirt and sport jacket and real trousers. He had grown up since I last saw him. My thoughts were rumbling around in my head, as I tried to concentrate on our conversation, still shaken by the day's service for my mother.

"Well, Lars, I'm here to take Lena back to her house. Nice to see you again," said Mrs. Lundberg as she began to steer me towards the door.

Lars stammered, "But, wait. I just offered to take Lena back to her house myself."

After a pause, not seeming to know exactly how to take this news, Mrs. Lundberg turned to me and asked, "Would you like that, Lena?"

I surprised myself when I blurted out, "Oh, yes, I would. Yes, Lars, thank you for asking. I would appreciate you taking me home."

"Now, you're sure, Lena, you feel well enough to stay by yourself in your grandmother's big old house tonight? You could come and sleep at my house, dear, if you wish."

"Yes, I'm sure. I'll be fine. I need some time to think. Thank you for all you've done, Mrs. Lundberg."

"Lena, we've known each other for a long time. Please call me by my first name, Sonja."

"Oh, yes, Sonja. Thank you for all your support." I was glad to drop the formality and be able to talk with Mrs. Lundberg, woman to woman. Maybe I could even get up the courage to tell her about the man I met in Paris, something I had not had the opportunity to tell my mother. I felt I may need some advice—I mean, should I encourage him, and how?

"Well, then, I'll say good night to you two young people. Thank you, Lars, for accompanying Lena back to her house. I'll check in on you in the morning, Lena."

"Tack," was all I could think to say, and all Lars

could say was, "Sure thing, Mrs. Lundberg. I'll see her safely home."

Lars took my arm by the elbow and kind of steered me out of the church reception hall to his car parked a short way down the hill. It was an old Chevy coupe, but in good shape. Lars seemed very proud to tell me he had fixed it up all by himself. "Got the engine running smoothly and now she purrs like a kitten," he said.

He opened the passenger-side door for me, and I slid into the dark-green-and-ivory vinyl seat, making sure to pull in my dress, the black one that had been mother's—appropriate, I thought, for a funeral. Lars went around to the driver's side, slid into his seat, started the car up, and off we went.

"Care to drive around a bit, Lena?" he asked.

"No, thank you, Lars. I don't feel really great. I would appreciate you taking me right home."

With a disappointed tone to his voice, Lars said, "Sure, sure, Lena. Glad to do that. I know right where your house is. Don't you remember how I used to watch you from the corner. I was too shy to ask you out then. Regret it now!"

"Oh, yes, I do remember that now." I was tongue-tied for a minute.

"Yeah, I liked you, Lena. You were the smartest girl in the school—and pretty, too." I saw the color pink rise behind the collar of his shirt, and knew he was blushing. I was, too. I didn't know quite how to take this compliment.

"Then I heard you went off to France. How was that, by the way? You goin' back?"

That was the first time I even thought about going

back to Paris. For the past two weeks, all I could think about was my mother and how would I survive without her.

"I'm not sure, Lars. I don't know if the college will extend my scholarship and if I can afford the travel back, but I would like to go back. Paris is wonderful and I'm learning so much there."

"Gosh, you sound really jazzed by it."

I wasn't quite sure what *jazzed* meant, but thought it must be good, and said, "Yes, I do love Paris."

As Lars pulled up in front of my house, he switched the car lights off and switched on the radio. I could hear the words to a song but was nervous and wondered what came next.

"Do you like Neil Young's 'Heart of Gold,' Lena? It's one of my favorites. He's cool." Lars reached over to my hand and tried to hold it.

I was startled and pulled it away. "I don't know that song, Lars, and besides, I better go in now." Frankly, the music didn't stir me like Charles Aznavour or Edith Piaf, two famous French singers I loved to listen to with Michelle at the cafes in Paris. Paris had changed me in just two short months.

As I was thinking this, Lars leaned over, trying to look into my eyes, and said, "Lena, will you see me again? Can I ask you out one night once you're feeling better after the shock of losing your mother?"

I pulled back from him slightly and said, "Oh, I don't know, Lars. Right now, I don't know what I'm going to do. But, yes, I guess you could call me in a couple of weeks." Part of me was flattered to have the attentions of a boy—well, young man—something I'd never experienced before. Well, on second thought, that wasn't exactly true. The French artist, Joseph, still lingered in my mind and how much more mature he seemed than Lars.

"Good. I'll show you up to the door, Lena," and before I could say no, thank you, Lars switched off the radio, got out of the car, and was around on my side helping me out, with his hand around my back.

We walked up the rickety old wood steps of Grandmother's house and Lars, only an inch taller than me, tried to kiss me at the door.

I turned my head away. "Lars, I don't know you well enough. Please, I have to go in now."

"Sorry, Lena, I just hoped we could become good friends. You're so beautiful and I've had a thing for you for a long time."

"A thing for me?" I wondered what that was. While Lars held the screen door open, I put the key in the lock and turned it, opened the door, then turned to him.

"Good night. Thank you for the ride home. I'm sure I'll see you before I go back to Paris."

With a crestfallen look, Lars turned to go. He looked back from the sidewalk and said, "I'll call you, Lena. Good night."

I waved and closed the door. With relief, I leaned my back against the closed door and let out a big sigh. The house seemed so quiet and the realization hit me. I'm alone! I remembered then how my mother had always said, "Lena, we Johanssons and Larssons are a strong bunch. Your grandmother, you, and I can get through anything."

• • •

Sometimes when we were so short of money, when all we had to eat were the apple dumplings that Grandmother made from the apples that grew on the tree in our yard, Grandmother would just remind us of the *old days*.

"Lena, just be glad we have the apple tree and good neighbors. We'll get through this." We were lucky if one of father's old friends dropped off a fish to fry. Grandmother was right. We had a kind community in Astoria. All the Scandinavians stuck together. I also recalled how Grandmother often told me about the Depression, how everyone pitched in and helped one another.

As I lay in my bed that night, after my mother's funeral, I remembered how, after Grandmother's funeral and cremation, Mother and I had vowed we would take Helga's ashes to Sweden together someday. That time would not come now; at least we wouldn't be going there together. I rose from my bed restless, not able to sleep. I slipped on the felt slippers Mother had left me. Pumpkin rose and curled around my legs as I walked to my bedroom door. He was getting old; it was harder for him to jump now, so he slept at the foot of the bed. Somehow, the slippers and Pumpkin's soft fur made me feel my mother was still nearby. I went to the kitchen with Pumpkin right behind me. Once there, I found the cupboard where Mother told me, just before she died, she had hidden the brass box with the ashes and a big mason jar with money she had been saving for our trip to Sweden. In the semi-darkness of the kitchen, the only light being the moonlight that streamed in through the window, I groped around in the cupboard. I found the box, pressed it to my chest, and then searched some more for the jar with the money. Sure enough, it was right where she said I'd find it. I set the box and the jar down on the counter, pulled the cord for the overhead lightbulb, went to the stove, and lit a match to light the gas burner. Then I put the kettle of water on the stove. When the kettle whistled, I poured the hot water into one of Mother's old chipped blue porcelain cups, which had really been Grandmother's, dipped a teabag in it, and waited until the tea was fully steeped. I held the teacup in one hand, the jar in the other, and shuffled to the table, where I sat down and just stared at the jar as I sipped my tea. Finally, I removed the brass-colored top, shook out the bills and change onto the table, and began to count them. I wanted to return to Paris, but how? How could I afford a plane trip back? The college assured me I could maintain my scholarship if I had the money to return. I slowly counted fifty, sixty, one hundred, two hundred, another fifty, two twenties, and ten ones. Maybe I would have enough after all—thanks to my mother's frugal saving. And maybe I could rent the house—yes, that might be it: my way back to Paris and then to Sweden. Tears welled up in my eyes as I thought of my mother's sacrifices. At the bottom of the jar was a folded piece of white paper on which mother had written a note.

Lena darling,

I may not be able to go with you to Sweden, after all. But please keep the dream. You must go and meet your Swedish Great Uncle and cousin. You must find out why Grandmother screamed at night – what was the dark secret she hid from us. Johann and Hanna will welcome you. His address is below. Write Johann

and he will give you all the directions you'll need. Your
Loving Mother, Sofia

I glanced back at the countertop where I had set
the brass box of Grandmother's ashes, wiped the tears
from my eyes with the sleeve of my terrycloth robe, and
vowed, under my breath, to return to Paris, finish my
studies, and then take Grandmother's and Mother's ashes to Sweden—somehow, someday.

With the help of Sonja Lundberg, I spent the next two
weeks interviewing potential renters. We finally settled
on a nice young couple, new to Astoria. He was a fisherman and his wife reminded me of a girl who had once
rented Grandmother's room, one of our first boarders. I
had liked her. The couple were so happy and promised
to take care of the house and Pumpkin, my aging cat,
too. I wasn't sure he would live much longer.

Before I left Astoria, after cleaning up the house
and storing all my personal items in a locked closet, I
walked to the beach where Grandmother had taken her
last steps. I thought of the lives in my family this rugged
Pacific had taken, my grandmother's and my father's.
Their deaths, and my mother's, were all written into my
heart, like a book of loss. I felt broken in half and wished
I had someone close with whom I could confide. I realized how alone I was. Could I rebuild a new life in Paris?
Would I find my roots in Sweden? I took one last look
at the vast Pacific and walked away from a dark past,
determined to overcome my childhood fears and rebuild
my own future.

A week later, I was again on a plane from Portland,
Oregon, bound for Paris, France.

Chapter 16

I tugged the heavy suitcases, two this time, behind me as I rolled them out onto the sidewalk outside the busy De Gaulle airport. At least I now understood how to get into the city by the RER, the fast train that ran from the airport to the center of Paris, within three metro stops from my residence hall. When I left Paris four weeks before, the old woman—Madame Grenier, with the garlic breath, who was the concierge of the residence—assured me she would watch over my room and make sure nothing was taken until I returned. I hadn't been sure I would ever be able to return, but I trusted the old woman and left all my books and the pretty dress Michelle had talked me into buying when we went shopping at the Galeries Lafayette. The dress was hyacinth blue, with a pencil skirt and a cowl neckline, sleeveless, and well, the sexiest dress I'd ever owned. "In fact," I exclaimed to Michelle, "I'll probably never have an occasion to wear it."

"Of course, you will, chérie. Just wait until the first Frenchman asks you out on a date. You'll be glad to have it!"

I wondered now if Joseph would remember me; it had been a month since we'd met. I collapsed onto the old lumpy bed and soon was fast asleep. In the middle of the night, I woke myself up with a scream. There was a tap on my door.

"Mademoiselle, Mademoiselle! *Vous êtes bien?*" The concierge was yelling through the door as she banged on it, asking if I was okay.

Startled by my own loud outcry, and shaking, I called out, "Oui, Madame. I just had a bad dream."

"Ah, bon—go back to sleep, my dear!"

The moonlight coming through the window cast a strange shadow across my bedcovers as I lay there, breathing hard, my throat sore from my straining it.

"I can't believe I did that," I whispered. "Don't tell me Grandmother's screaming is contagious!"

I got up and poured myself a glass of water, went back to bed, and wrestled with sleeplessness all night until it was time to get up and prepare for my class at the Sorbonne. I looked forward to seeing my friend Michelle again.

• • •

As I ran up the steps of the Sorbonne, I almost ran into her. Our timing was perfect.

"Ah, Lena, you've returned to Paris. Bien venue! I'm so happy to see you. Just between you and me, I think Professor Michaud will be too."

"Oh, I'm sure he doesn't even know who I am, Michelle. Why do you think he has missed me?"

"In class one day, he read from one of your papers and commented it was from one of the American students. He pointed to the empty seat where you always sit and said the piece was by Mademoiselle Larsson and 'très bon.' You see, Lena, he does notice you."

I felt the color rise in my face and was undeniably pleased to hear that my writing, at least, met with approval from the professor.

Just then he rushed past us. He looked back at me: "Well, well, Mademoiselle—nice to have you back. I hope it won't be too hard for you to catch up after your sojourn in the US."

I felt my cheeks grow hot, and the sting of tears coming to my eyes as the professor turned his back and went towards the lecture hall.

"Oh, don't pay any attention to him," said Michelle. "He's just being an arrogant Frenchman. I know he truly admires your writing. Come now. We have to get to class on time."

After class, Michelle and I went for a coffee at the nearby sidewalk café where many of the students hung out. She asked me about my mother, and I had to give her my sad news. I was tearful as I recounted the story of my mother's death and my sadness that we would never go to Sweden together to meet our relatives.

"But you can still go, Lena," said Michelle. "I'm sure your uncle and his family will welcome you. They will be interested in hearing about your life in America and about what you are doing in Paris. Come on, cheer up. Winter break is coming up and it's not too expensive to take the train—just a long trip, I think. It might be very good for you now, Lena—get your mind off your great loss. By the way, my boyfriend asked if you ever got to the art studio he recommended."

Absentmindedly, I stirred my café au lait with the small teaspoon the waiter provided and nodded. "As a matter of fact, I went there just before returning to the States."

I didn't know if I should tell Michelle about Joseph, the man I'd met there. I probably would never see him again. Best not to bring him up.

"Did you like it?"

"Oh, oui, very much. I hope to go back there."

"Bon," said Michelle as she got up. "I have to run now and meet Jean Jacques. *Au revoir et á bientôt!*" She dropped a couple of francs on the table as a tip for the waiter and ran off.

I was touched by Michelle's concern and desire to help me, but, at the same time, I was not sure about her suggestion to go and draw again. I wasn't sure I even knew how to draw anymore. I hadn't picked up a drawing pencil and sketched since that day at the studio, which now seemed so long ago. I lingered a bit longer at the café, while I munched on the roasted chestnuts I had bought from the corner vendor and finished my coffee. I walked slowly back to the residence. Outside the main entrance I rang the concierge bell. I had forgotten my key.

Madame Grenier pulled open the door and motioned me to enter. "Oh, *mon dieu*, child. You had me very worried last night with that loud scream you let out. Are you sure you are OK?"

"Oui, Madame. I think I just had a bad dream."

"Well, I certainly hope that doesn't happen again. We'll have to send you to a doctor."

"Excusez-moi, Madame. I have to hurry and pick

up my drawing materials. I'm going to an art studio to sketch." On the way back to the residence, I'd remembered it was Wednesday—wasn't that the day Joseph told me he was always at the studio?

"Well, well, and then what are you going to do about your studies? I'm sure you have fallen behind—being gone for a few weeks."

I slipped past Madame Grenier and climbed the circular staircase to the third floor, waving as I passed the old woman. Leaning over the banister, I called out, "Don't worry, Madame, I'll be fine and will keep up with my studies. I promise!"

"Old busy body," I whispered to myself—actually, though, I had to admit that Madame Grenier reminded me a bit of my beloved grandmother.

Chapter 18

That day, when I returned to the atelier, I almost tripped on the steps ascending from the metro as I hurried to get to the studio on time. Just as I reached the black door, I ran headlong into Joseph. He didn't realize it was me, and when I dropped my hat, he picked it up and said, "Oh, Mademoiselle—excusez-moi!"

Embarrassed, I grabbed the hat from his hands, breathless, as I felt the blush rise to my face. I couldn't think what to say. It didn't matter. Joseph filled in the silence.

"Lena—you see I remember your name. I'm delighted to see you. I was almost sure you would never return to the studio. After the third week I stopped looking for you. I hope I can convince you this time to go with me for coffee after our drawing session."

I nearly melted as he looked at me with his intense dark eyes, which seemed so sincere. I finally found my tongue and was just about to accept his invitation when Monsieur Louis yelled impatiently, "*Allez, allez-vous.* Go on in—you both can pay me later."

I ran ahead of Joseph and took the same seat as the first time I was there. There were more people this time. Joseph had to sit several seats away. I could hardly concentrate on the model, this time a male—small and thin, but with nicely defined muscles. Joseph glanced over at me, and we caught each other's eyes several times during the session.

Though wary, I felt myself falling under a kind of spell he seemed to cast over me. I knew I would go to coffee with him. I told myself: After all, how can I expect to have a love life, which I've longed for, if I always say 'No' at the first advance? I may miss my last chance.

Though I had no aspirations to be a professional artist, I was enticed by the fact that he may be a gallery owner. I remembered the calling card he had handed me the first time we met: Galerie Bleu, it said. I was curious.

It didn't take long for me to fall head over heels for Joseph, six years my senior, interesting, clever, and with a history that fascinated me. Joseph was a bit shorter than I, maybe by an inch. That didn't bother me in the least—his handsomely carved face, dark eyes, and gentlemanly ways were far more important to me. He was of slender build, a fine dresser, and knew just the right thing to say to put me at ease. I wondered how many girlfriends he had. I couldn't help comparing his savoir-faire to the awkward advances of Lars, back home.

By our second date, I wrote in my journal that his dark eyes were so intense, I sometimes felt they would bore holes through mine as we stared at each other over a glass of wine. Yes, I was even drinking wine now, not to bury my sorrows, more to improve my French.

Joseph said my French was much better when I relaxed. The wine helped. I began to think I might be falling in love, whatever that was supposed to feel like. Mother had never discussed that with me, and, of course, neither had Grandmother. Weren't the Swedes known for being believers in *free love*?

Joseph's family history was interesting to me, too. He was Jewish. His grandmother had escaped the pogroms in Russia and come to France, where she'd married a successful businessman. His mother, the only child of the Russian woman, grew up in Paris, became an artist, and finally married a Frenchman, owner of Galerie Bleu. Why, he even knew Picasso. When the Vichy were in power and France was under the influence of the German occupiers, his mother and father fled France and lived in England where Joseph was born, just six years before me. He had an older brother who died during the war. Joseph was not only fluent in French and Russian, but spoke nearly perfect English, having had an English nanny and started school there.

His parents had cousins taken by the Vichy regime during the war and sent to concentration camps. Listening to his parents talk about this when he was a small boy had affected him profoundly. He could truly empathize with how I was impacted by the trauma of Grandmother's nightly screams and her ultimate suicide. He knew what it was to suffer loss. We had no communication problems—none, that is, until I began to suffer from nights of anxiety and worries about how I would ever get to Sweden to finally find the answers to Helga's secrets and bury the ashes, as I had promised my mother I would do.

On our third date, when I yawned incessantly

through the magnificent ballet that Joseph took me to at the Opéra, I was so embarrassed. Over coffee afterwards, Joseph said, "Lena, I hope you will take this in the right way, chérie. I think perhaps you might benefit from seeing a therapist about your sleep disorder, obviously brought on by all the trauma you experienced in your childhood."

At first, I was aghast at Joseph's suggestion. "Joseph, do you think I'm crazy?"

"No, of course not, Lena, but psychiatrists are not just for crazy people; they can help you discover for yourself what is lurking in your subconscious, perhaps something from your past that might cause you to behave like you do, to awake often at night, and to even perhaps cry out on occasion. My family has a friend, a very good therapist. I encourage you to see him. He has helped my mother, who suffered the trauma of loss."

I had been biting my nails, a habit I had not broken. Embarrassed, I dropped my hands to my side as he turned to embrace me before saying good night. With his gentle persuasion, I finally agreed to make an appointment to see Dr. Lanier, the psychiatrist.

Chapter 17

I dragged myself to class for the next two days and put off taking Joseph's suggestion. Finally, on the third day, when I hadn't slept well for three nights in a row, I found Joseph's calling card under my door with the phone number for Dr. Lanier and a note: "Lena, chérie, call him. You will feel much better. *Bises*, Joseph." That last affectionate word, "kisses," did it. I walked back down the stairs to the *rez-de-chaussée* where the concierge lived and knocked on her door.

"Oui?" I heard Madame Grenier's gravel-like voice call out from her inner sanctum. "Oui? Who is there, s'il vous plaît?"

I answered, "C'est moi, Lena. The student who woke you up with my loud cry a few nights ago."

At that, the door flung open and she seemed happy to see me. I knew she was nosey and maybe thought she could get more juicy details out of me—why I had screamed that night from a bad dream, who the young man was she directed to my room. Joseph, of course. I wasn't about to tell her.

"Madame, may I please use your phone for a moment? I need to make an appointment."

"Well, yes, if you'll keep it short. You know, I pay by the minute. Entrez-vous."

Madame Grenier led me down a short but dark hallway to her living room. The place reeked of garlic and the carpet felt sticky on the soles of my shoes—she was always chewing on something and most likely dropped crumbs wherever she walked. Her large old grandfather's clock that took up one corner of the living room rattled my nerves with its steady tick-tock, like the beating of my heart.

"Merci for allowing me to use your phone, Madame, I said."

"Did you say you were calling to make an appointment?" She held a napkin and wiped some food from the corner of her mouth with it. "What kind of an appointment? With a doctor? I hope you're not ill."

I knew her curiosity was provoked—she was waiting for me to tell her who I was calling or thought she just might stay there and listen in to what I was about to say.

There was an awkward moment when neither of us spoke, but I wouldn't gratify her nosiness.

"No, I'm calling for a friend," I lied.

"Well, I'll just go back to the kitchen and finish my dinner."

I picked up the telephone receiver and dialed the number Joseph had given me. After three rings, a man's deep mellow voice responded.

"Oui? Doctor Lanier here."

Before he could say more, I jumped in with my most, I hoped, articulate French. I explained that I was

Joseph's friend and asked to make an appointment.

"Ah, oui, Mademoiselle Larsson. I've been expecting your call." He continued in almost perfect English. "Joseph told me you might be calling to make an appointment. I have Wednesday at 4:30 open. Will that work?"

I was so surprised by his English, I paused for a minute.

"Mademoiselle, are you still there?"

"Ah, oui, Doctor Lanier. Wednesday would be great. I have a class at 3:00, my last for the day and your office is not far from the Sorbonne. I'll be there on time."

"*Parfait*, Mademoiselle! *Et puis*"—he slipped back to his beautiful and lilting French—"*nous avons un rendezvous, le mercredi à quatre heures et demie.*"

The phone clicked and I knew he had hung up.

I pondered a moment; 4:30 on Wednesday would mean I would miss my drawing session at the art studio where I usually met Joseph. He had become my main motivation for my weekly rush to the studio. I loved drawing from the model, but sitting next to Joseph made it even better, feeling his arm brush against mine as he furiously tried to capture the pose of the model. The two of us looking up at one another and then back at our drawing pads, comparing our sketches after the pose ended, I always feeling his was better—all this made Wednesdays a highlight of my week.

Now I would miss that, but looked forward to shedding my fears, to unleashing my story of my grandmother and her ultimate suicide. I knew I had to find the key to her secrets and her dark past, not only for myself, but for Joseph if I was to have a relationship with him. Maybe Dr. Lanier could help.

The day of the appointment arrived. I was nervous all day but told myself over and over that this was a good way to start untying the knots of my life. I knew Grandmother's past was somehow interlocked with growing up, shy and nervous. It did little to make me more confident in myself. Loss of my mother had only pushed me deeper into self-doubt and despair.

That Wednesday, I took a shortcut through the Luxembourg Gardens as I walked to Dr. Lanier's office. When I arrived, I saw there was a brass plaque on the door that said: Dr. Robert Lanier, Docteur de Psychologie. I rang a bell and heard a click as the ancient wooden door opened. I entered with some trepidation. It was quiet inside. There was a long hallway carpeted with an oriental rug. At the end of the hallway, a door opened, and I could see light emanating from the interior. A tall, attractive older man, perhaps in his fifties, dressed in casual sweater and slacks, walked towards me. He took my hand in his for a brief moment, then invited me to follow him into his office. The room was dimly lit, pleasantly appointed with a Louis XV desk and chair, an antique armoire to one side, and a dark brown upholstered leather chaise with a headrest at one end, where he motioned me to lie down, or—

"Please. Sit, if you wish," he said.

I set my backpack down and sat, with my hands tucked between my knees, pressed together to avoid shaking too much.

"I have to admit, Dr. Lanier, I'm a bit nervous. I've never been to a psychiatrist."

He smiled. "That's normal. Don't worry. You'll soon relax. Now, tell me your story, Lena. How can I help you?"

"Well, I guess Joseph may have told you that I often cannot sleep, and I sometimes wake up from nightmares, occasionally waking myself with a loud cry."

"And what do you think causes those nightmares," asked Dr. Lanier.

"When I was a child, my father died in an accident at sea. In fact, I was only a few weeks old, still an infant. I never knew him. He was a fisherman. Then my grandmother came to live with us, with my mother and me. Grandmother was a Swedish immigrant. She often screamed at night, and ultimately, she committed suicide." I paused, feeling the sweat on my back and my hands as I began to shake again, my shoulders tense.

Dr. Lanier spoke: "I would say, Lena, that may be a very good reason for you to find it hard to sleep and to wake with anxiety. Awakening to the screams of your grandmother frequently during your childhood may have very well affected you deeply, and her suicide also. Were you close to her?"

As Dr. Lanier helped me to uncover my life story of growing up a shy girl in a family dominated by two strong women and without a father, he guided me to the realization that I needed to know more about my grandmother, about the things she kept secret and why. The things that ultimately led to her suicide.

At the end of our third session, Dr. Lanier said, "Lena, I would suggest, it would be helpful for you to go to Sweden, as you tell me you and your mother often discussed, to meet your only remaining relatives. I believe you said that your great-uncle Johann is still living and may be able to share with you the trauma your grandmother suffered in 1939, during a visit. Is that right?"

"Yes, that's what Mother thought."

"She was right. The secret your grandmother would not disclose may be the key to your ending the cycle of trauma. You need to know what happened to her in 1939 to drive her to take her own life—what demons she lived with up until then. This may very well help you."

• • •

In spite of Dr. Lanier's advice, I was reluctant to leave Joseph. Maybe he would forget me, find some other young woman who met his fancy more than me. There were enough pretty young French women to meet, though admittedly, I noticed not too many went to the atelier to draw. The models usually stayed very aloof from the artists. In fact, some of the most interesting models were many years older than Joseph or I. Their more mature bodies, and even slightly wrinkled skin and wizened faces, were the most provocative to draw. They had character, as Mother might have said.

Deep down, I knew Joseph was right. Dr. Lanier, too, and I had made a promise to Mother. I wrote Johann and Hanna that I may be coming to Sweden during my winter break and waited to receive a reply.

A week later, as I was on my way to Professor Michaud's class, I ran, unexpectedly, into Peter. I hadn't seen him since our meeting outside the bookstore, before my return to Astoria and my loss of Mother.

"Bonjour, Lena. It's good to see you. I thought you may have dropped off the edge of the earth." He laughed in that same lighthearted manner he had at the bookstore. He reached out to shake my hand.

"Oh, Peter, it's good to see you again," I said. "I'm on my way to a class."

"Can I take you to coffee afterwards?"

"Why, yes, that would be nice." I was anxious to talk to someone about my decision to go to Sweden, but my doubts, also. Joseph had told me he had to go to England for a week to do some art-related jobs for the gallery. I was on my own to make the plans.

"Good, then, after your class? Is four o'clock alright? I'll meet you at the Café Roland near the Sorbonne. Do you know where that is?"

"Oh, oui," I said. "My friend Michelle and I sometimes meet there. Tack, see you then."

We waved good-bye, and I went to my class, nervous but excited to have run into Peter.

• • •

The final straw, the incident that convinced me I had to go to Sweden sooner than later, happened that day. Professor Michaud was delivering a recitation on Baudelaire when my head nodded off. I awoke with a start when I felt a tap on my shoulder. The professor stood at my side where I sat in an aisle seat. He glared down at me. He had tapped me on the shoulder with the stick he used to point to various phrases he scrawled on the blackboard for the students to recite. It was my turn.

"Wake up, *réveillez*, Mademoiselle Larsson. You may leave this class immediately, and don't come back until you can stay awake during my recitations. That's final!"

Dazed and embarrassed, I grabbed my books, thrust

them into my blue canvas backpack, stood and ran from the class, humiliated. Outside the closed doors of the lecture hall, I leaned against the grey stone wall of this venerable institution of learning, brushed the tears from my eyes, took a deep breath, and whispered to myself, "That's it, I'm going to find out the answers—what happened in 1939 and why Grandmother committed suicide. I'm going to Sweden!"

I was so upset I nearly missed my appointment to meet Peter. Perhaps he could, in fact, help me with my plans. I had no idea how far away Sweden was from Paris, which trains I would have to take from which station. I hurried to the café, and there Peter was, waiting at a table just inside the door. Though Michelle and I often sat outside, I was relieved that Peter had chosen an inside table. The late fall air was getting nippy.

Peter stood as I entered Café Roland. "Bonjour, Lena. Let me take your bookbag and set it here under the table."

I sat down, breathless, still upset over what had happened in Professor Michaud's class. I proceeded to tell Peter about the incident. He had a serious look on his face and was a good listener. Finally, I came to the end of my story, lowered my head, so he wouldn't see the tears that welled up in my eyes.

"Gee, Lena, that's not a very happy story." He reached out and touched my hand, which rested on the table. To my surprise, I didn't pull it away. For some strange reason, Peter almost seemed like a brother to me. I don't know why. He was handsome and could be a close second to Joseph, but I liked having him as a friend. Of course, we did not know each other at all well yet.

Peter ordered two coffees as the waiter rushed by with a full tray he was taking outside.

"Oui, Monsieur."

I proceeded to tell Peter my fears about going to Sweden and to ask him if it would be a long and difficult journey.

"No, not at all, Lena. Well, yes, by train it does take a number of hours, but it's not difficult. You'll have to make one transfer, I think, in Copenhagen and then on to—what is the name of the town, did you say?"

"Ronneby," I replied.

"Well, I live in Stockholm, which is north of there, and when I go it takes me about two days. I usually stop in Amsterdam overnight. I have a friend there. It's roughly 1600 kilometers to Stockholm from Paris, but, of course, Ronneby is not far from Malmö, and that's in the south, so it shouldn't take near that time. How about if you go with me tomorrow. I have to go to the station to pick up my tickets, as my family wants me to come home for the holidays. I will be leaving right at the beginning of winter break. Perhaps we can even share part of the trip together."

I felt a huge weight of worry slip from my shoulders. "Oh, Peter. That would be great! I'm afraid, though, I am a big disappointment for you. I don't speak much Swedish, only a few words from Swedish nursery rhymes my grandmother taught me."

Peter's blue eyes lit up and he whistled under his breath. "Gee, Lena, that's a shame you don't speak Swedish, but I can't wait to hear those nursery rhymes." He broke into a smile. We laughed and suddenly I felt more assured about my upcoming trip.

"Do you know the Christmas poem about the

tomten, the little gnomes?" I asked.

"Sure, of course, I know that one—every kid in Sweden learns that. Don't worry about not knowing much Swedish. Lots of Swedes speak English. You'll get along fine, and if we travel partway together, I can teach you a few words and expressions."

The waiter came by with our coffee, and Peter and I made our plans to meet the next day to go to the train station and buy our tickets. I knew now I would keep the promise I had made to Mother.

Part III

Sweden 1974

Chapter 18

At the last minute, Peter's plans changed. He decided not to go back to Sweden in spite of his family's wishes. A friend at the Sorbonne invited him to go skiing in Chamonix, a reportedly beautiful ski resort. He couldn't resist the invitation. So, I would be making the trip to Sweden alone. Maybe it would be a good time for me to map out my strategies, how I would ask Johann for more information about 1939 and Grandmother. I was worried. Hanna, Johann's second wife, had written that Uncle Johann was very ill and that I should come as soon as possible. I wondered again if I was doing the right thing. Leaving Joseph, just when our romance seemed to be budding, and turning down an invitation from Michelle to visit her family in the south of France.

I boarded the train on a Saturday night. Joseph was unable to come to the station with me as he was away on a business trip for his father's Galerie Bleu. He promised to be at the station to meet me when I returned. I was filled with doubts and trepidation. Maybe Johann would be too ill to talk to me, to answer my many questions. Maybe he didn't have a clue as to why Helga had nightmares.

With a loud lurch the train pulled out of the Gare de l'Est in Paris. I settled back in the stiff leatherette seat and looked out the window. Tile-roofed houses, industrial sites, and rocky embankments sped by in a blur. The train's wheels made a clickity-clack sound as they rolled over the track towards my destination— southern Sweden. Questions and doubts flew through my head like the blur of the passing scenes outside the train's windows. I wondered what lay ahead. Would it be a troll under the bridge or a good fairy bringing me all that I sought—all I needed to know about Grandmother's past? I remembered Grimms' fairy tales Grandmother often read to me when I was a child. Their endings were often grim—enough to wake me up from my sleep almost as often as Helga's nightmares.

As the train rattled along, I looked out again as we whirred past the outskirts of Paris and into the countryside. My face was reflected in the window. It was misty outside, raining. I thought of Verlaine's poem—the metaphor for one's sad heart being like the rain falling on the city. Soon, I grew tired and lay my head back on the white-cotton-covered headrest and fell into a deep slumber.

• • •

I don't know how long I slept; all I know is that I awoke with a start when the train lurched to a stop. I almost resented having to leave my dreams; in some ways, they seemed much better than my current reality. We were stopped at a station on the border of Belgium—I don't remember the name. I was lost in a fog of memories elicited by my dreams as passengers brushed past me with their suitcases and rushed to depart the train, others just boarding. An older man with a long nose and glasses looked at his ticket then glanced down at me.

"*Pardonnez-moi*, Madame. Please don't let me disturb you, but I believe I have the seat next to you."

Still half asleep, I said, "Oh, no, not a problem." I hastened to move my backpack, which I had set on the seat beside me when I boarded the train.

The gentleman lifted his briefcase to place it in the luggage rack above our heads, then sat down and began to read *Le Monde,* his newspaper. A loud whistle of the train blared as it started to chug its way northward. I slipped back into a kind of trance of memory. I knew it was going to be a long journey, with a brief stopover in Amsterdam and then on to Denmark and my destination, Ronneby Station, just a short distance from Malmö, Sweden, in the region Grandmother always called Skåne. It always seemed important to her that we knew we were from the south of Sweden, once under the control of Denmark. She'd tell me that the Skanians, the name for people of that region, were very proud people, different from those from Stockholm and the north. I never understood quite why. Now all I wanted to do was try to remember that last two weeks in Paris when I met Joseph and, well, felt like I was falling in love. As I looked out the window of the train, I could almost see his handsome face reflected there, smiling back at me. Soon, I drifted back to sleep. Several hours later the train once again lurched to a stop. I saw that my seatmate had disappeared and left his newspaper on the seat beside me. *Le Monde's* headlines read:

CRISE de L'ENERGIE.
Le président américain Nixon demande des réductions
de la consommation de pétrole.

My French was just good enough to understand the words. President Nixon was facing an energy crisis and demanding that all Americans cut back on their oil consumption. Never having paid a lot of attention to the daily news before, I realized now how important world events were. I wondered how this would affect my small community in Astoria. Would my renters have enough heat to warm the upstairs bedrooms? I was now a landlord and would have to think of those things. We had an oil furnace along with the wood-burning stove. I made a mental note that, once I arrived in Sweden, I would have to make a long-distance call to Sonja Lundberg and make sure all was well.

Worried about the news, and thinking about my arrival in Sweden, I couldn't really sleep more, so I unzipped the top pocket of my backpack and pulled out the three black-and-white photos, the ones Grandmother had ripped from her album, wrapped in her handkerchief, and left for me to find in her dresser drawer.

It was hard to make out the photos' details in the dim light of the night train's compartment. I fingered the photos and tried for the one hundredth time to figure out the answers to the questions that plagued me: what did these people mean to Helga, what did they have to do with Grandmother's screams at night and her decision to take her own life? The first photo was of a towhead little girl, her hair glistening in the sun; Mother said that was her at age five, when Grandmother Helga took her to Sweden in the summer of 1939, the year that Europe was on fire as Hitler threatened to march into Poland. Next to mother was a boy of an undetermined age—older, but not by many years. Mother said she thought he was her cousin, the one born with some type of mental disorder, a bit "slow" was all she knew. He would have been the son of Grandmother Helga's brother, Gunnar. He was handing the little girl a bouquet of flowers—yes, they were daisies. When Grandmother first turned to that photo in her album, all she would say was his name was Axel, but Mother said Uncle Johann had changed his name to Axel. Why, I wondered. The other photo was of Uncle Johann, Grandmother's other brother, standing next to Rebecca. I remember how Grandmother always brought her handkerchief, the one that now cradled the photos, to tear-filled eyes when she saw that photo and whispered, "Johann's wife, my sister-in-law, Rebecca. Poor thing." Next to Rebecca stood Grandmother Helga, in a plainer dress, but pretty, with blonde hair, golden like mine. The two women had their arms around each other. As I studied that photo, I brushed my finger across a fourth figure, someone I hadn't noticed in the photo before—or maybe I had but grandmother refused to talk about him. He was stocky and towheaded and stood in the shadows, behind the other three. Yes, that's right. That's the photo that most agitated Grandmother.

The night was misty, the sky like a charcoal drawing with white puffs as clouds. I could see my reflection in the train's window. My cheeks were wet, like the moisture that had collected on the window. It still rained outside. The sound of the train's wheels droned on: clickity-clack, clickety-clack.

As I studied the photos more, I remembered how Mother had said that all she knew was that that photo, too, had been taken the year that Grandmother went to Sweden in 1939. Grandmother hadn't seen her brothers since she had immigrated in 1917, nearly twenty-two years before. Of course, Mother didn't remember anything of their visit in 1939—she was too young. All she knew was that Rebecca, Johann's Jewish wife and a musician, had mysteriously died of some kind of stomach disorder, she thought, during the time of Grandmother's visit. I had heard this story over and over, but there seemed to be a missing link—several, in fact. From what did Rebecca die? Why did Grandmother dislike her brother Gunnar? How and when did Gunnar die and leave the raising of his son to Johann? Where was Axel's mother? The questions rolled around in my mind like dice in a roulette wheel; I had seen one in a Hollywood movie with a gambling scene. Going to Sweden now was my gamble, not knowing if I would find the answers I sought.

I mulled over these thoughts and recollections as I leaned my head back again. I curled up my knees under me, pulled my heavy knit sweater around my shoulders as the motion of the train lulled me back to sleep. I dreamed I had fallen off a high precipice only to land in the depths of the unknown, a deep pool of darkness. My hands still clutched the photographs.

Chapter 19

Several hours later, I awoke with a start when the train once again lurched to a stop. The photos had slipped from my hands and fallen to the floor. Just as I went to reach for them, the conductor came by to announce that the next stop was Copenhagen, where I was to get off and change trains to one that crossed the Sound by ferry to Sweden. The conductor stooped to pick up my photos and handed them to me.

"Did you drop these, Miss?"

"Oh, yes, thank you." I was relieved not to have lost them. "Are we almost there?"

"Indeed, we are, Miss, almost to Copenhagen. Your ticket shows you will get off there and take another train on to Ronneby, Sweden. You slept through our stop in Amsterdam."

Twelve hours? How could that be? I asked myself. That was the most I'd slept in ages.

The conductor smiled, tipped his hat, and continued to the next train car. I glanced one last time at the photos and then slipped them back into the outside pocket of my canvas backpack, zipped it, and looked out the window to a landscape totally different than that of France.

As we left Copenhagen, I peered out at low rolling hills of lush green dotted with small red-roofed houses here and there, like toy villages, and eventually deep forests of birch and alders.

Just a little over two hours later, the train pulled into the Ronneby station. There was a large crowd milling around the station platform. I looked out the window and strained to see if I could identify Hanna and Axel. Hanna had sent me a photo and explained she and Axel would be waiting on the platform in front of the station when I arrived. Axel would have on a red hat.

Worried that I could not see them, I scanned the crowd again. "Oh, there they are," I said to myself, under my breath. In the midst of the throngs of people, I saw a stocky woman in a grey overcoat, with a dark blue felt hat on her head. Next to her was an equally stocky man, slightly taller, and with, sure enough, a red knitted cap with black-and-grey earflaps pulled down over his head. The two were stretching their necks as they gazed at the train. I grabbed my backpack and walked quickly down the aisle to the train's vestibule, where I descended onto the platform. I waved at the woman and man I felt sure were Hanna and Axel. They finally caught sight of me and pushed their way through the crowd on the platform, towards where I stood. Breathless and excited, we all shook hands.

"*Välkommen,* Lena! Axel and I are happy you finally made it to Sweden. Let's get out of this crowd."

"Oh, Hanna, I'm so glad, too, to finally be here," I said.

Axel took my arm and looked at me with a broad warm smile.

"Don't you have any suitcases, my dear?" asked Hanna.

"No, just this big backpack filled to the gills. I like to travel light, and since I thought it might be cold, I just wore layers of shirts and sweaters. See the one I have on is my very warmest; Grandmother Helga knitted it for me when I was only fifteen, just before she died. She made it extra big and said I would have to grow into it. Well, it fits perfectly now."

Hanna laughed. "That sounds like your grandmother. I remember her to always be a very practical woman. We used to play together, you know, when she, Johann, and Gunnar were children. When she came back so many years after she immigrated to America, I saw she still had a feisty spirit and was clever, but practical, too. She sure adored your mother, the baby she had waited so long to have. Follow me. Our car is parked over there." Hanna pointed in the distance to an old Volvo, light blue in color. The three of us headed in the direction of the car, holding our heads down against the bitter cold wind.

"Well, Lena, you're arriving in Sweden where it sometimes seems we never see enough of the sun until our long days in the summer. It's cold, but, you'll see, *ve* have our own beauty here."

She opened the car door, and Axel got in the back seat. He set my backpack down beside him and wrapped an arm around it as if to protect it. Hanna motioned for me to jump into the front while she went around to the driver's side and settled in, barely fitting her plump body in behind the steering wheel. Embarrassed, she said, "Johann always cautioned me not to eat too much or I might not be able to fit into the car. Ha, *vel,* he was right. It's hard to resist the *kakar*, I admit, and holiday times are when I bake. Axel likes the sweets, too."

Hanna started the car and pulled out of the parking lot behind the station.

"Since it's getting late, Lena—you must be tired after your long train ride—we won't show you the town now, but wait until the daylight. Best we get you home and to bed after filling your tummy. Did you eat anything on the train?" Without waiting for my answer, she said, "You must be hungry."

"Oh, yes, a little. I did have a *sandwich jambon,* I mean a ham sandwich, I brought from Paris and an apple. Oh, and some chocolate," I said, "but I could eat a little. I can't believe I slept almost the whole trip. How is Johann?"

Hanna didn't say a word for a long while and seemed to be concentrating on her driving as she took a narrow road out of the town and followed it for several kilometers. There was an awkward silence in the car, and then she finally said, "*Vel,* Lena, I'm sad to say, Johann passed away three weeks ago, right after I sent you the post card. We had the funeral and burial shortly after. I'm sorry you didn't make it in time to meet him. I know he looked forward to meeting you. He left a note for you."

Stunned—and terribly disappointed—I finally found my words. "Oh, Hanna, I'm so sorry, too. My sympathy for you and Axel."

It was quiet in the car for the rest of the way to the

farm. I fidgeted with the yarn ties that hung from my wool cap and thought to myself, Now I may never find the answers I was seeking, those that perhaps only Johann could have provided. I wondered when Hanna would give me Johann's note. As happy as I was to have arrived, I felt let down and depressed by the news.

Soon, Hanna drove the car by a forest, which edged both sides of the road. That must be the Blekinge woods that Grandmother Helga often talked about, I thought. As we rounded a bend in the road, Hanna swerved the car down a narrow lane, past a big field, and then pulled up in front of an old house and came to a stop.

"Ya, well, we're here, Lena," said Hanna. "Valcommen to the Karlsson farm."

Karlsson was Grandmother Helga's mother's family name. Her father and mother had inherited the land years ago, before Helga was born. I remembered Grandmother talking about that—saying at least owning some land put them a step above some of their neighbors.

Axel jumped out from the back seat and began to unload some bags from the trunk of the car. I peered out my window, curious about this place where my grandmother had once lived. The house was painted the typical red of so many houses in that part of Sweden and trimmed in white gingerbread-like designs. The paint was worn, and the building looked worn, too, having survived three generations. The steps leading up to the front door sagged a little, but all around the house were beautiful shrubs and birch trees, dusted with a light layer of white. I felt a chill in the air, the dry white crispness of new snow.

As if she read my mind, Hanna said, "Ya, it snowed

a bit last night. Johann always liked the snow; he said it was nature's way of giving the plants and animals a rest before they reawakened in the spring. Well, I guess that's one way of looking at it. But for me, it just makes things a bit harder, like getting the goats and the chickens in out of the cold, buttoning down the hatches, so to speak. Now, let's go in and get you some food. Axel will bring in your backpack."

Dazed, I followed Hanna up the steps to the outer door, which entered a mud porch. It was like the ones some old houses in Astoria had. There was some carving on the door—symbols of some sort. There was also a black satin bow tacked to the door. I realized it was a sign of mourning for someone who had recently died—my great-uncle Johann.

Hanna explained the symbols were carved by Johann's father—Viking marks. "Speaking of that," said Hanna, "see over there just beyond the bend on that small hill, that's an old Viking burial site." She pointed to a small hill a few hundred feet from the house. "We'll take you on a tour tomorrow. Come now, you're tired and hungry."

I strained to see what Hanna was pointing at, but couldn't make out the details, only that there was a mound and what looked like enormous stones at the top.

Through the oval window in the door from the mud porch, to the house's interior, I saw a parlor-like room to the right of an entry hall. It looked warm and cozy inside. Hanna began to take off her coat, scarf, and woolen hat and hung them on a row of brass hooks across one wall of the enclosed porch. She sat down on a bench and motioned me to do the same.

"You can leave your hat and boots here, too, Lena," said Hanna. "Just put on those wooden clogs." She pointed to a pair of not-so-comfortable-looking clogs. "Then, follow me to the kitchen. We'll show you the rest of the house tomorrow."

Axel had gone ahead and lit a fire in a fireplace in the parlor and brought some wood into the kitchen, too.

"Axel helps me a lot now, especially since Johann left us. He's a good boy, even if his father was not," said Hanna.

I wondered at this last remark. Mother and Grandmother always maintained that Johann had raised the son of Gunnar, who, Grandmother said, had left Sweden during the war. When I'd ask about Axel's mother, Grandmother would just say she died and then brush aside my questions and change the subject. I knew this was part of the mystery I had to uncover. I also wondered at Hanna's referring to Axel as a good boy. He appeared to be in his forties, a bit older than my deceased mother. I felt like Nancy Drew, the sleuth. I loved reading her mystery books when I was a child.

Too shy and weary to ask too many questions of Hanna now, I hoped, in the coming days, I would have the opportunity to discuss Gunnar and the photos Grandmother had left me. Perhaps I had lost my last chance to learn more with Johann's passing, but I hoped Hanna would be able to provide answers to my many questions.

• • •

"Come, now, Lena, tell me what you would like for supper. I've made some cabbage soup with meatballs, and we have *bröd* and butter, some goats cheese and fruit. Will that do?"

"Oh, Hanna, that sounds delicious; thank you so much," I said as my stomach grumbled. I hadn't eaten since the apple on the train the previous night. "I feel sorry to think you and Axel have had to prepare for my visit at such a sad time, just after Uncle Johann passed away. My apologies I didn't arrive sooner when I might have helped you."

"No, child, that's not a problem. But do tell me why your late mother and you wanted so badly to talk to Johann. He read me one of your mother's letters, and she said something about needing to clear up what happened those many years ago when your Grandmother Helga visited with her as a small girl." Hanna paused. "In fact, I remember that visit. I don't understand what she meant by 'clearing up what happened.' For one thing, it's so many years ago, I don't think Johann, nor I, could remember anything really significant. I was the housekeeper then. All I remember was your grandmother's beautiful smile, golden hair, and the joy she showed in being little Sofia's mother. I guess she waited a long time for that baby girl, after losing her first one. Your mother was such a darling child." Hanna turned to say something in Swedish to Axel. I guess it was about my mother, whom he played with so many years ago. Axel's eyes brightened and he shook his head with enthusiasm.

There was a long pause. The two of them just looked at each other and then Hanna turned to me and said, "At least the first month of her visit, there was a lot of joy in the house. Your grandmother loved getting to know Johann's wife, Rebecca. Ya, she was a beauty alright, and your mother and she hit it off from the beginning. It was sad when Rebecca became ill. No one quite understood it—she died so suddenly. Well, let's talk about more pleasant things now over our meal."

These remarks raised even more questions for me. There seemed to be so much mystery around the "unexpected" death of Rebecca. I knew that must have been a part of Grandmother's despair.

"Axel, while I dish up the food, why don't you take Lena's backpack up and show her the room we prepared and the WC where she can wash up a bit."

I noticed that Hanna spoke in Swedish whenever addressing Axel but used fairly good English when speaking to me. I made a vow to try to remember some of the Swedish Grandmother and Mother had taught me.

Axel looked pleased as he picked up my backpack he had set down by the door and motioned for me to follow him up the stairs.

"Tack, Axel," I said as we climbed the stairs, covered with old, worn carpet. Once on the landing, Axel opened a door to a room cast in shadow now as the night's moonlight filtered through the lace curtains at the one dormer window. It was a modest but comfortable-enough room. Against one wall was a big double bed covered with a light blue duvet. There were two white bath towels lying at the end of the bed. The pillow shams were of a Marimekko fabric in yellows and blues. My mother had loved sewing with Marimekko prints when she could find them. Sitting on an antique side table was a porcelain vase with fresh flowers. On another wall, next to the single window that looked down to the front of the house, was a three-drawered dresser painted bright lemon yellow. The room felt cozy and warm.

Axel set my pack down and pulled open a drawer, motioning that I could put my clothes there. Then abruptly he left the room and closed the door.

I flopped down on the edge of the bed, removed the clogs that Hanna had given me in the mud room, and looked in my backpack for my slip-on ballerina shoes, as I called my soft French slippers. Oh, it felt so good to slip my feet into something comfortable. I took my hair brush out of my backpack and brushed my hair, plaiting it into a long braid, then left the room and descended the stairs. I could hear Hanna bossing Axel around in the kitchen and headed down the hall to join them.

The three of us sat at a square table with a yellow cloth on it and more of the same flowers I had in my room. The table was laid out with plates, cups and utensils. Hanna dished up the cabbage and meatballs, passed the basket of bread, and then sat down with a sigh.

"Well, ya, you are finally here, Lena. We hope you'll stay with us through Christmas."

I nodded and said, "Well, I hope I can. That will depend on what I can discover about my grandmother's past, Hanna. I hope you'll be able to help me."

Hanna laughed. "Lena, that's many, many years ago when your grandmother was here. I'm not sure I can remember much from those times, except that they were hard—ya, very hard. It was just before the war in Europe, you know."

"Yes, that's one of the things I want to talk to you about."

"Well, let's do that tomorrow after you've had a good night's sleep, Lena."

"That's one of the problems, Hanna. I have a very hard time sleeping. I hope I won't disturb you and Axel if I'm awake most of the night. I like to write in my journal when I can't sleep. You see, Grandmother Helga screamed often in the night and woke Mother and me. We thought perhaps there's a connection between why I suffer from insomnia and my childhood memories of Grandmother's ear-piercing cries at night."

"Ah, that is it. I don't remember Helga screaming while she was here, but she did have a hard time after Rebecca died and then Gunnar disappeared."

"Wait, Hanna, I thought Gunnar left to go and fight in the war—that's what Mother thought, too."

"Well, we don't know exactly. We'll talk about it tomorrow," said Hanna. With that, she rose from the table and began clearing the dishes. Axel had been very quiet during this conversation, but seemed to take a cue from Hanna's remark. Maybe he recognized his father's name. He rose, smiled at me with a nod of his head, and walked out the back door.

I was bewildered and hoped I hadn't said anything to offend Axel or Hanna. My first impression was that he did not understand English. I asked Hanna, "Did I say something to offend Axel?"

"Oh, don't mind him, Lena. He likes you," said Hanna. "I can tell that. He just goes out at night to check on the goats and chickens and to bring more wood in for the fire."

"May I help with the dishes?" I asked.

"Oh, no, you are tired after your travels. Why don't you go up to your room and get settled? I'll bring you a cup of coffee and some sweets soon."

"Thank you, Hanna, but I don't drink coffee at night—it makes falling asleep even harder for me."

"Ah, ya. Vell, run along now. I'll see you in the morning. Ve talk more then."

Chapter 20

The next day I explored the farm, alone at first while Axel and Hanna were occupied with chores. I began to get a feel for the simple but hardworking life that Hanna and Axel led. Hanna explained about how hard they had to work to raise enough potatoes and rutabagas to put away for the winter provisions, how the chickens and goats helped to provide them with income. They sold eggs to locals and also made goat cheese in the small red shed Hanna pointed to near the fields. They sold some garden produce, too, at the local weekly market in Ronneby. When they finished their chores, Hanna told me about the neighbors and promised to take me into the town of Ronneby and show me where my great-grandfather's blacksmith shop had been. She explained it was now a coffee shop.

"We could stop for *kaffe och kakor,*" she said. I noticed she spoke a mix of Swedish and English and wondered who had taught her English.

She laughed when I asked. "Oh, Johann thought it very important that I learn English. He said I had to become 'more cultured'—that is what he said. Of course, his late wife Rebecca was multilingual, not only pretty but very cultured. So, I try now for you. I hope you can understand me. Axel and I noticed you speak a little Swedish, Lena. *Det är bra.* You noticed, I'm sure, Axel understands only Swedish, but occasionally he can pick up a word or two in English, words which I've taught him. We will get along fine, won't we?"

Over lunch, I tried several times to ask Hanna more about Rebecca and how she died, and more still about Gunnar, but every time I started to talk about the past, Hanna seemed anxious to change the subject.

Finally, on my third day at the farm, I felt I might be on to something when Hanna took me to see the large stones with the runes, the ancient Viking markings, on them. This, she said, was a Viking burial ground. Hanna explained that Johann always revered their Viking past. She went on to say, though, that after Rebecca died Johann never went back there. I didn't exactly know why this caught my attention, but it did, and I wrote it down in my journal. I was keeping notes to track the answers I got to my questions, an old trick I'd learned from some spy novels I'd read—ones Mrs. Olsen had recommended for me to understand plot and scenes.

On my fourth day at Johann's farm, I finally got up the nerve to try again, to ask Hanna some more questions. We were having coffee at the wooden table in the kitchen.

"Hanna, I've been wondering about some things that might have taken place while my grandmother was here in 1939."

"Ya, your grandmother was fun to be around, and

your mother, little Sofia, was such a cute child." Hanna put down her coffee cup, looked out the kitchen window as if remembering those days so long ago. "Ya, I know you're curious about that time, Lena."

"Yes, I am," I said emphatically. "Well, I mean, I need to know some things. My grandmother, Helga, you know, as I said, used to scream at night. At least once a week I heard her. As you can imagine, it was very scary. Mother and I never understood why, but sometimes we wondered if she had bad memories of something that happened while she was visiting here shortly before World War II."

Hanna brought the corner of her cotton apron up to her eyes and wiped them quickly, turned away, got up, and walked to the sink with her coffee cup, as if reflecting carefully on what she might say next to me.

"Well, Lena, now that you ask me, ya, I do vaguely remember some things, in fact. Just three days before your grandmother left on the ship to return to America, something strange did happen. I remember now."

Hanna returned to her seat, and I leaned in close towards her, over the table, and stared at her, waiting almost breathlessly for her to continue.

"Oh, please go on. Tell me what you remember—this is terribly important to me."

"Well, dear, it's a long time ago. You know at that time I was not married to your great-uncle Johann. I worked for him—and Rebecca—as a maid. Of course, I had known him for a long time, as our families were neighbors. We played together as children. Johann, Helga, and I, sometimes Gunnar. I had always admired Johann—and later, of course, his beautiful Jewish wife."

I sensed something odd about, "of course, his beautiful Jewish wife," as if she felt it necessary to add, as an afterthought. It almost felt as if she meant to avoid any suspicion that she felt any differently about Rebecca than she did about Johann. I wondered, was she jealous of Rebecca? Had she hoped it would turn out differently, that Johann would marry her?

"Please, Hanna, please go on. Do you remember more? What happened that you can recall?"

Hanna continued slowly, choosing her words with care. "*Ya, väl,* Johann seemed anxious one day. He walked up and down the hallway upstairs. I could hear his footsteps as I worked in the kitchen. Of course, you know he was grieving deeply over the sudden death of his wife, Rebecca."

"Yes, but what happened then?" I pressed.

"I seem to recall that your grandmother was out walking with little Sofia. She, too, was fraught with grief over Rebecca's death. The two of them, your grandmother Helga and Rebecca, got along very well from the start, as I've said. Their brief friendship was cut off when Rebecca died."

"Why do you suppose Johann was pacing? Do you remember more?" I moved my chair closer to hers, anxious to hear more details, and rubbed my sweating hands together in my lap. "Please, Hanna, go on."

"Well, soon Mr. Johann—that's what I called him in those days; Rebecca felt it more polite—he came downstairs and walked out the door straight for the old shed next to the field. I could see him, through the kitchen window, as he ran out there. It was late afternoon. Just then your grandmother walked in with little Sofia and went upstairs to lay her down to sleep. She left the house shortly after and headed to the shed, where Johann was. I was finishing up my chores here and preparing to leave for the day."

Hanna hesitated, her brow furrowed. She rubbed her forehead as if trying to coax the memories back.

"Ya, ya, that's it. Johann went into the shed and didn't come into the house for a long time. When he finally returned, he still seemed agitated. I recall thinking he smelled of something—something pungent— and finally realized it was the mushrooms, the ones we sometimes collected in the forest, the ones we later threw out knowing they were poisonous, ones in the Amanita genus; we call some the 'death cap' mushrooms, not good to eat."

"Why do you suppose he smelled of the mushrooms," I asked, confused, but intrigued by this bit of information."

"I don't know—it's funny. I just remember thinking it was odd. I guess I concluded he was merely separating them from the good ones he had collected before he brought them to me to cook." Hanna paused. "Yes, that's it."

Why was I feeling that Hanna was making this up as she went?

"Then what?"

"Well, yes, the next day, in the afternoon, I think, towards dusk, is when I heard the scream from the field."

With the word scream, my back stiffened, and all I could think about were Grandmother Helga's cries in the night that made me bolt from my sleep as a child. I felt a chill vibrate through my body and opened my eyes wide to stare at Hanna. Beginning to shake, I said,

"Please go on."

Hanna fell into a long silence, then stood up, walked back to the sink, and began to wash the coffee cups. She peered out the window as if looking towards the farm fields. I could see her trying to control her hands from shaking.

She turned and glared at me. "Oh, Lena, I'm tired and can't remember more. Why don't you go for a walk? It's nippy outside. Put on your woolen hat and jacket. We'll talk more later."

I knew I had pushed Hanna, maybe too much. I would have to stop interrogating her now for a while, give her a chance to rest. Maybe, just maybe, she'd remember more tomorrow—I hoped.

I spent the rest of the day writing in my journal. As I lay down on the bed in my room in the late afternoon, my mind wandered. I felt homesick and also missed Paris and Joseph.

There was a sudden sound downstairs that woke me from my daydreaming. I could hear Hanna saying something to Axel in a strong, almost scolding, voice, but the words were not clear. I saw that it was now dark outside. My stomach growled. I glanced at my watch; it was ten o'clock at night. Should I go downstairs and ask Hanna for a snack, I wondered. Finally, I got up, pulled on my slippers, and walked out into the hall. Hanna had just slipped into her room across from mine. I wondered where Axel slept. I walked softly down the carpeted stairs, and in the dim light I could see into the parlor across the hallway from the stairs. There, curled up in a big blanket, lay Axel on the couch. I realized he had given up his room for me. I quietly walked down the hall into the kitchen, peered out to the shed that

Hanna had been looking at after we ate, and wondered: what was it about the shed that drew her attention?

The moon rose in the east, big and round, its rays piercing the dark like an unsheathed sword. Did something happen that night of the scream when Hanna prepared to leave. Was she trying to avoid my questions? Tomorrow, I would have to explore more and try to get some answers. For now, my stomach growled. I spied an apple and took it up to my room, ate it, and began once again writing in my journal all that I knew so far. I thought I was careful not to wake anyone, but I was to learn the next day that I was not careful enough. The next morning as I arose from my bed, I could hear Hanna and Axel again in the hallway. She seemed to be giving him instructions, perhaps just his chores for the day. I hoped I would have a chance to thank him for giving up his room for me. I wanted to spend more time with him—alone. He seemed like a gentle soul, somewhat lost and lonely, though, of course, he had Hanna to look after him. Since I had arrived, he smiled often at me, his eyes crinkled like those Swedish elves, tomten, in the stories Grandmother told me when I was a child. But he said little, just making a few sounds from time to time, sounds I could not make out.

I dressed, pulled on my heavy woolen socks, hoping to go for a walk in the woods nearby, the ones Grandmother called the Blekinge woods near their farm. As I descended the staircase, Hanna looked up and said, "Oh, there you are, Lena. Axel and I were just talking about what we would do today. We thought you might like to see your grandmother's old school, and then we'll go into town to see the blacksmith shop; as I already told you, it's now a coffee shop. We'll stop and have that kaffe and kakor I promised you."

"Oh, I'd love that!" Down deep I had really hoped to spend some time alone with Axel so I could tell him how much I appreciated his giving up his room for me. But how would I say that so he could understand. I didn't think I remembered enough Swedish. It was obvious, too, that Hanna dominated him and our schedule.

"Come now. I've got breakfast ready for you and then we'll leave," said Hanna.

We spent the day driving and walking around Ronneby, stopping for coffee and cakes at the place that once was my great-grandfather's blacksmith shop. It didn't look like a blacksmith shop now. Hanna also introduced me to some of her friends, mostly in the shops and markets where she sold her goat cheese and vegetables. The day went by quickly. Hanna gave me little chance to continue my interrogation.

That night Axel joined us for dinner. I was beginning to feel more comfortable with this gentle but somewhat strange, silent man with the big ears and piercing blue eyes, who behaved more like a child than a full-grown man, always seeming to see and understand more than he could express. He spoke little, and when he did it was in hesitant murmurs. Hannah explained that he was always like that from the time he was a small boy, a bit "dimwitted." I winced at the word Hanna used—dimwitted. My hunch was that Axel was a lot smarter than she thought. He was like a child in a man's body, sweet and gentle, but intense at the same time. Something stuck in my head—he's not at all dimwitted; I think he knows something.

Hanna dished up the Swedish meatballs and

potatoes. They reminded me of those that Grandmother Helga used to make. Axel seemed to relish them and kept helping himself to more. I could just make out a few words of Hannah's in Swedish. "Now, Axel, you've had enough. You know what your Uncle Johann used to always say. You'll get a fat belly if you eat too much; your eyes are larger than your stomach. Remember?"

Axel looked down as if ashamed and continued to pick at the rest of the food on his plate.

I wanted to change the subject to avoid Axel being any more embarrassed than he probably already was. "Hanna," I ventured to ask, "do you remember more of the story you began to tell me yesterday morning—I mean about when my grandmother Helga was here?"

Hanna wiped the corner of her mouth with the light-blue-and-yellow checkered napkin. "Well . . ." She looked a bit anxiously over at Axel, as if fearful to say something that might upset him. Then, in Swedish, she said, "Axel, you've eaten quite enough—why don't you go out and feed the chickens and put the goats in the bedding shed?" My Swedish was slowly coming back and I could understand much of this, especially her body language as she shook a finger at Axel and motioned him to leave.

Like a small obedient boy, Axel pushed his chair back, stood up, picked up his plate and utensils, took them to the kitchen sink, and then, with a wave to me, he turned to walk out the back door, his coat and his hat in his hand.

"There now, we can talk more freely," Hanna said. I didn't understand why Hanna said this or why she sent Axel away, but I was anxious to continue the conversation.

"Yes, what more do you remember, Hanna?" I shifted in my chair. Hanna seemed more nervous and began to scrape her fork back and forth on her plate, moving her remaining meatballs around slowly, as if playing a game. She looked up at me, almost as if she was looking through me, back to the past.

"Well, what I remember after that scream I heard that afternoon was that Gunnar never came back."

"What?" I exclaimed. "But why—what do you think happened to him?

"Johann said that Gunnar decided to move back to the village where Axel's mother lived, to move back in with her, that they had reconciled and that we would be taking care of young Axel. I admit that it didn't quite make sense to me, but I was willing to accept anything Johann told me. You see, Johann was like a Viking god to me, ever since we were children and played together—I, well, Lena, I loved him."

There it was—the admission. I sucked in my breath and let it out slowly as I waited for the next admission—or maybe a confession. Something told me this was a clue, a revelation I shouldn't ignore, but I didn't know why yet. Did Johann know Hanna loved him. Did Rebecca? Was there some jealousy there? I was groping in the dark for answers.

I continued, "But why do you think Johann would say that. That seems strange, I mean coming up so suddenly."

"It did to me, too, but I didn't feel it my place, at that time, to ask any more questions."

I was puzzled. "Well, go on. Was my grandmother still here when all this took place?"

"Ya, she was, though after that day of the scream

from the fields, until the morning she left, I saw little of her. She stayed in her room with your mother. I remember we expected her to stay all summer, but Johann said she was missing her husband, Olaf, and was returning sooner to America. He said she was busy packing, preparing for her departure. Who was I to question Johann, my employer? Two days later they left together, all three, to drive to Malmö where Johann said good-bye to her at the boat docks, when she boarded the ship back to America. Axel, who was then only six, seemed upset and cried a lot. He often went to the Viking burial ground to play. I thought he acted as children do when they have a secret, but I never knew what it was. You know children like him can imagine things."

I felt confused and anxious at these revelations—what was Hanna suggesting? What happened that morning a couple of days before Grandmother Helga and my mother, her small daughter, departed from Sweden? What was the significance of the hill and the Viking burial ground? Why did they have so much significance for Axel? I remembered the first morning after my arrival when I peered out the lace-curtained frosted windows of my guest room in the dim morning light. I saw Axel wandering towards the hill near a large pond.

"It's late now; why don't you get some rest, Lena. We can talk more tomorrow. I want to show you around the village some more, and maybe you would like to buy a souvenir or two to take back to Paris."

"Oh, yes, that's nice of you," I said, but down deep I thought to myself that the only souvenir I wanted to take back was the solution to my sleepless nights and the knowledge that I had finally uncovered Grandmother's secrets, as I promised Mother I would do. I vowed to try to learn where Gunnar had moved, how far away the village was. Maybe I could go there, meet the family of Axel's mother, if they were still there. In fact, maybe, just maybe, his mother was still alive. After all, Axel was six in 1939. It was now 1973, and he must be forty. His mother surely could not be older than maybe sixty or sixty-five, depending on when she gave birth? If I was lucky, I would find her, and she would have the answers. That, at least, was my hope.

Hanna's deep, guttural voice broke through my thoughts. "Lena, Lena, wake up." She reached over and tapped my shoulder gently, as if trying to wake me from a hypnotic trance. It reminded me of Mother, how she used to pat me to wake me up from my daydreaming, or at night, after one of Grandmother's outcries, to help me go back to sleep. I missed her.

I startled. "Oh, I'm sorry, Hanna. I was lost in thought." I felt my face turn hot, and I was sure it was red with embarrassment. I fidgeted with my napkin and began to sweat.

Hanna continued. "You seemed as if you were far away."

"Yes, I guess I was. I admit, I still have so many questions."

"Well, my dear, I think I've told you all I can remember," said Hanna. "You know I'm an old woman now, and my memory is no longer as sharp as it used to be. Let's talk more tomorrow when we go on our shopping excursion. I think you're very tired."

I could not shake off the nagging feeling at the back of my mind that Hanna knew more than she admitted, but I agreed to end our conversation for now.

"Yes, I didn't sleep well last night. I think I'll turn in early. I want to write in my journal before I go to sleep. Would you mind, Hanna, if I don't help with the dishes tonight? I promised Axel I'd go for a walk in the Blekinge woods tomorrow morning to gather mushrooms." I made this story up, remembering how I had seen Axel bring in a basket of mushrooms a few days before.

Before Hanna could answer, Axel appeared. He had slipped back into the house by the back door and was standing slightly behind the door into the dining room. He seemed to understand what I had just said to Hanna, but how? There was something terribly endearing about him as he smiled broadly at Hanna and me, and said, "Ya, ya, Lena" as he pointed in the direction of the woods. I could finally make out a few of his hesitant Swedish words. He was like a child in a man's body. Hanna seemed surprised. "Well, I guess that would work. You can both go and gather the mushrooms for tomorrow's supper. Then we can go into town for our shopping. Ya, that's OK."

"Well, then, I'll go up to bed now and wish you both a good night. Or, as Grandmother used to say, God natt."

Axel took off the dark knitted cap he always wore and tipped it to me with a bow. Hanna stood and began to remove the dishes from the table. Axel helped.

"Fine, Hanna said. We'll see you in the morning at breakfast. Sleep well, dear,"

As I mounted the creaking old stairs, I mused about the evening's conversation. I knew I had to find out what really happened to Gunnar. To Rebecca, too. Somehow the two seemed connected, and I knew it was by more than Johann's marriage to Rebecca. Something in my bones told me this might be the clue to my grandmother's bad dreams and to her secrets.

Chapter 21

The early morning sunlight came through the window and stroked my cheek, barely visible under my puffy goose-feather-filled duvet as I peered through half-closed eyelids, not wanting to fully waken. No longer able to sleep, though, I threw the duvet back, rubbed my sore eyes, and stretched. At least I had slept through the night for the first time since my arrival in Sweden. Perhaps it was because yesterday's conversation with Hanna had begun to offer me some clues—a path forward. I could hear the chickens clucking in front of the house and the loud rooster crowing his good-morning song. I liked these sounds. They were different than the deep foghorns I heard when I awoke in Astoria, or the church bells that I had become accustomed to in Paris.

I rose slowly, then walked to the window and looked down to see Axel looking up in the direction of my room, as if anxious to go for our walk. I waved to him, turned to go to the bathroom in the hallway, where I splashed cold water on my face, brushed my teeth, and combed my hair. I quickly pulled it into a pony-tail and returned to my bedroom to dress. I pulled on my blue jeans and my big hand-knitted warm sweat-er with Scandinavian motifs across the front—it was another that Grandmother Helga had knitted for me not long before she died. It still fit my skinny frame. I hadn't changed much in those years: oh, acquired small breasts and grew another inch or two—that's all. I sat down on the edge of the cushy bed and pulled on my high-top leather boots. I would need them, as there was still snow on the ground from the first day of my arrival when it came down in gentle drifts. The last thing I grabbed was the knitted cap, the one I wore on the train and loved so much because it reminded me of Grandmother. Under my breath, I whispered to my mother, who was always in my thoughts: "See, Mother, I'm keeping my promise—I'm in Sweden and I'll find out Grandmother Helga's secret, and then both you and I can rest in peace." As I said this, I remem-bered that I must ask Hanna where I should scatter my mother's and grandmother's ashes. I had both with me. I brushed aside a single tear and walked out of the room, confident that today I would learn something new. Excited, I skipped, rather than walked, down the stairs to the front door.

Hanna stopped me in the entry hall. "Lena, aren't you going to eat some breakfast before your walk in the woods? Axel has already had some porridge."

"Oh, yes—I saw him out my window waiting for me," I said. "That's why I was hurrying. I don't want to keep him waiting long."

"Never you mind, Lena," said Hanna. "He'll wait a bit longer. Axel is very patient. Come and have some coffee. Take off your hat, or you'll get your death of cold when you go out.

I laughed at this remark. "Yes, Mother used to say that—'one should not put a hat on while inside, or they will catch a cold when outside.' I remember that well." I pulled off my hat and followed Hanna into the kitchen where she had laid out some hot rolls, a plate of herring, some fruit, and a cup of coffee.

"Will this be enough, Lena?"

"Yes—way too much, in fact. I'm sorry, but I do not eat herring." I grimaced at the memory of the first time Grandmother had forced me to try this traditional Swedish delicacy. I gagged and then threw up all over the kitchen floor of our Astorian house. Grandmother got angry with me, saying, "All Swedish people like herring." How could I ever forget that?

"Well, eat what you can, Lena," Hanna said. She sat down opposite me, poured the coffee from the dented, old silver pot into the slightly chipped blue china cups, of the same pattern as Grandmother's.

"I hope you slept better last night, Lena," said Hanna.

"Ya, I did—much better, thank you."

"Gut," said Hanna.

We sat quietly as we munched on the rolls and drank our coffee. Then Hanna looked me straight in the eyes and said, with a serious tone in her voice, "Be careful when you're in the woods with Axel. He knows the forest well and will watch out for you, but don't believe everything he says." I couldn't help feeling that this was strange, as we both knew Axel didn't talk much, and, when he did, it was in fits and starts, hard to understand. Hanna knew, though—somehow, instinctively—that he was smart. Was she afraid he knew things she didn't want me to know? I looked forward to spending more time with Axel alone.

"Oh, don't worry, Hanna. I look forward to our walk. Grandmother Helga often spoke of her love of walking in the Blekinge woods, gathering mushrooms for her mother, then rowing on the pond. She said she could only do this the rare times when her father allowed her, as most days he needed her to help him at the blacksmith shop."

"Ya, Johann often talked to me about what a taskmaster your great-grandfather was. Johann did not like his father much and was glad when he could escape to Prague to study his violin. Did you know that is where he first met his Rebecca, the Jewish girl he married?" (I wondered why Hanna always made reference to Rebecca's Jewishness; it seemed to me she held some kind of misgiving about that—could it be she had some kind of distaste for Jews? Prejudice, I knew, could sometimes reveal itself in subtle ways. I remember even in our community of Astoria the Finns sometimes did not like the Swedes and vice versa. Also, there were profound dislikes of the Chinese at our school. This always bothered me. Afterall, they built our railroads and contributed to our country in many other ways. Mother agreed with me.

I wanted to know more about Rebecca, but I could see Axel jumping up and down, waving at me through the kitchen window, his face anxious. I set my cup down and began to grab my wool hat. I could tell it was cold outside by the frost on the window.

"To answer you, Hanna, no, I never knew much about how Johann met Rebecca. I really want to know that, but I can see Axel is quite anxious for me to start our walk. Please, may we talk about that later?"

"Yes, my dear, of course. You're right. You better leave now. Remember we want to go shopping in the village later, so don't be gone too long. We have only a few hours of daylight here this time of year, you know. Wait. I'll give you a basket for the mushrooms."

Hanna went to a small closet where she pulled out the mushroom-collecting basket. It was wire mesh, trimmed in wood, with a worn wooden handle. She handed it to me and said, "Now be sure you let Axel show you which are the good mushrooms. Be careful—many are poisonous. He knows."

"Tack, yes, I'll watch which ones he picks out. Don't worry. We'll be back in time to go to the village," I said.

Once outside, Axel gave me a big smile and pointed in the direction of the woods. The two of us set off at a fast pace in the crisp chill of the morning. I could see our breaths in front of us as we walked briskly, side-by-side. The sky was bright blue in spite of the cold. I felt excitement at the prospect of going to the woods that Grandmother had so often spoken to me about—one of her favorite places.

I could see the tree line across the end of the field. As we entered the woods, the light dimmed due to the dense overstory. Heavy stands of fir, beech, ash, and birch, clustered together; the ground was covered with deep mounds of moss and dotted with stones, all dusted with white snow, like powdered sugar. Miniature birch cropped up between the rocks, and all was wet with dew and melting patches of snow. Axel was almost childlike as he jumped and skipped along, totally familiar with this landscape—like a wood nymph in his own beloved environment. Through the trees the morning sun cast its light and tree shadows played on the ground.

Suddenly, Axel grabbed my hand. I laughed and he did too. It was like we were children. Maybe he was remembering what it was like when he played with my mother, so many years ago, when they were both children. Then his expression changed, and he pulled harder on my hand as if he was anxious to show me something.

"*Komma*," he said, pointing to a small clearing of light in the dark forest. As we approached, I could sense Axel's anxious determination.

He pointed to a stone, larger than the others where we had been running and different in shape. This stone was tall and flat, standing upright, much like the bigger stones on the hill Hanna said were carved with Viking runes, symbols suggesting an ancient burial ground, not far from the house. It was obvious this stone was a marking, too, placed there on purpose.

The stone stood at the head of a mound, the length of a human body, which was covered with decomposing plant material, mostly fully composted, as if it had been neglected for years. Next to that mound was a fresher one, a bit longer but with no stone. It was covered, too, with decomposing flowers. I could even make out a few petals, maybe roses, asters—I wasn't sure. It was obvious that we were at another burial site, one much older and another more recent. Axel was agitated and continued to point at the mounds. Then he knelt down and wrapped his arms around the stone on the older site. I squinted to read the faint lettering carved into the stone. My Swedish was not good enough to understand it all, but the name Rebecca stood out to me, plainly.

For a moment I was still with surprise, then let out a short breath and turned to Axel: "Ya, Axel," I said in my stilted Swedish. "I see this is where Johann's first wife, Rebecca, was buried. Is that what you wanted to show me? Is the other mound where you and Hanna buried Johann?"

Axel looked up at me with an earnest expression and shook his head ya. Tears began to flood his eyes.

"You must miss him—Rebecca, too. I remember Grandmother said Rebecca died while she was visiting here in 1939 and that you and my mother, Sofia, were just young children. I know my grandmother was very fond of Rebecca." I said this partially to myself and wasn't really sure he understood me.

Axel stroked the stone, touched the earth gently, then looked up at me again. He shook his head in a gesture of no, no. I tried to understand what he was attempting to say.

"*Nej, nej gut.*" I finally realized that Axel was telling me something in Swedish that I could understand. Something, he said, was not good.

"Do you know how she died, Axel?" I ventured to ask, still hoping I could solve the mystery of her death. I mimicked dying by slumping to the ground and lying very still, then looking at him in a questioning stare, shaking my head.

Axel looked confused for a moment; then, as if a magic light bulb went on in his head, he brushed aside some vegetation at the bottom of a nearby tree and held up a mushroom. At first, I didn't understand. He motioned to the mushroom and then to his mouth and made a grimacing face. Something began to dawn on me.

"Are you saying Rebecca ate mushrooms that were *förgifta*, Axel?" I remembered one time when Grandmother had tried to warn me about taking some medicine she had in her room by her bed. She had said it would be poisonous, *förgifta,* for me.

Axel shook his head yes over and over and looked down as if deeply troubled.

"But how? By accident? *Olyka*? My Swedish was coming back to me more and more.

Axel shook his head no and again looked down at the gravesite, agitated. He threw up his hands and shook them as if frustrated he could not tell me what he knew.

"Are you trying to say someone gave her the mushrooms, Axel? She was poisoned by someone? But who would do such a thing?"

Axel shrugged, looked down and shook his head again, sad.

As I asked this, an appalling truth began to unfold for me and sink into my psyche. But who would do this? Is this why Grandmother screamed—did she know the truth of this and could not bear it? I began to get excited that I was on to something—something really important.

"Go on, Axel. Please try to tell me or show me more," I said, hoping somehow he understood.

Axel began to pull me in another direction, towards a small lake, more like a pond, not far from the house and close to the Viking burial hill. Geese took flight over the water as we approached, flapping their graceful white wings as they headed off in a southernly direction. The water glistened in the early morning sunlight. I saw an old wooden boat tied to a leaning wood dock. The boat was half sunk in the muddy rim of the lake. Tall grasses nearly hid it.

Was Axel trying to tell me something about the pond? But how did that connect to Rebecca's and Johann's burial site? I was stymied trying to put it all together. I knew Axel was searching for something he could not articulate. He made guttural sounds I could only partially understand. Then he abruptly turned and looked up to the distant hill and ran, dropping my hand and motioning me to follow. I could tell he was anxious. I began to feel anxious too, afraid of what I might uncover.

"What are you trying to tell me, Axel? Was this Johann's boat? Did someone drown?" The minute I asked that, I knew it could not be right. I remembered that Grandmother said Rebecca died of a stomach disorder, a mysterious sickness that took her life in just a week's time. That matched with the thought she was poisoned by mushrooms, but why then was Axel anxious to show me the Viking burial ground again? Why the pond? Questions flew through my mind as fast as I ran to keep up with Axel. Axel grabbed my hand again and continued to run quickly. I almost tripped on my own feet. "Please, Axel, slow up. I can't keep up with you. Besides, aren't we supposed to be gathering the mushrooms Hanna wants for dinner tonight, the chanterelles?" I pointed to the basket and tried to make him understand, but he was on a mission to show me something important, and all I could do was follow. He motioned for me to follow him up the steep hill to the burial site. We had made a full circle from the field to the woods and back a slightly different route, by the pond. We were almost back to the main house. Then something very strange happened: Axel lay down on his stomach next to the largest stone, grasped it, his arms not able to surround its whole girth. He looked up with tears again as he had done at Rebecca's gravesite. But this time he let out a deep sob.

I was aghast. I did not know what to do or how to react to Axel's sudden, and what seemed to be irrational, burst of emotion. How could I comfort him? "I'm not sure what you're trying to tell me, Axel, but I can tell you feel sad. Are you sad about the ground where the Vikings were buried hundreds of years ago or what? What do you want me to know? Please, I want to understand.

Axel tried, with his guttural sounds and partial Swedish words, to express something to me, something I felt deep down was very important. I struggled to understand him.

"*Far, Far*" were the only sounds I could make out. Wait—I sucked in my breath and said softly to myself, "*Far* is the Swedish word for Father." Axel had lost his father, Gunnar, like I had. But how and when?

Axel heard me, and his eyes lit up as he rose and wiped his tears away with the sleeve of his heavy wool jacket and shook his head up and down as if to indicate, "Yes, that's right."

"Axel, is your father, Gunnar, buried here—is that what you are trying to say?" Axel shook his head furiously, again mouthing, "Ya, ya."

I searched my memory, struggling to remember exactly what Grandmother had said about her brother Gunnar, the one it seemed she had not liked. She had never said much. Instead, she seemed intention-ally to avoid talking about him when we would come to a photo that I was pretty sure was her brother—not Johann, but the other one. All she said once was that he joined the military and went off to war. But that never made sense to me. I knew Sweden declared neutral-ity during the Second World War. Grandmother never received any letters from Gunnar, only from Johann. Mother and I could only assume he was dead, but how: in the war or by something much more sinister. Why would he be buried here under the sacred Viking burial stone marked with the runes? As I pondered, mysti-fied, Axel grabbed my hand again and led me back to the woods. He seemed more at peace now, as if he had had a mission that he'd accomplished; something he'd wanted me to know had been revealed, but instead of answering any of my questions about that summer of 1939 during Helga's visit, this information just deep-ened the mystery and added to my anxiety. I vowed to think about this later, write it down in my journal, and try to piece it together to make sense of it. Now Axel and I had a task to complete for Hanna—pick the mushrooms for tonight's supper.

As Axel and I ran back to the woods, I felt the sweat under my thick sweater run down my arms. I was glad when he finally stopped and began groping under trees and rocks, digging his fingers into the moist rich com-post and pushing aside small plants to uncover the winter mushrooms. He finally found a nice mound of them, pulled them out of the soft earth and held them up to my nose, then pointed to their undersides. "Oh, I see what you're trying to show me, Axel. This is how I should identify the mushrooms we want to collect for Hanna, right?" I pointed to my eyes and then the mushrooms and made a positive sign with my thumb.

Axel shook his head and smiled. "Ya, ya!"

We proceeded to gather the mushrooms and soon the basket was brimming with the soft brown fungi with the slightly sweet earthy smell. I pointed to my watch and then in the direction of the house, trying to let Axel know that we better get back to the house now, that Hanna would be waiting for us.

Axel seemed to understand and nodded his head in agreement. We walked arm in arm with the basket back to the house. I was growing more and more fond of this dear man, my second cousin, once removed. I told myself I would ask Hanna as soon as I had the chance about the significance of Axel's actions. What had he been trying to tell me about his father? About Rebecca? Surely, she would know—more than she had revealed so far, or maybe more than she wanted to reveal.

Chapter 22

Hanna was anxious when we came back to the red house, so pretty in amongst the trees still lightly powdered with snow. Icicles hung from the white gingerbread eves. We stomped the snow and earth from our boots and walked in through the back door to the warm kitchen where Hanna waited.

"*Det är bra*. You're back in time. Looks like you found the good mushrooms, the winter ones, not quite like the chanterelles, but still tasty." Good job, Axel. Like a small boy receiving kudos from his parent, Axel looked proud, smiled and pointed at me.

"Oh, no, don't give me the credit. Axel found far more than me, Hanna. He's a good mushroom hunter."

"Ya, he is that—knows how to identify the safe ones to eat. Many are poisonous, you know."

For some reason, her statement stayed lodged in my brain—something to think about later. This was the second time she'd made mention of poisonous mushrooms. Why was it significant? I didn't know yet.

"Now, come on you two." She spoke to us as if we

were her children. I didn't mind but rather enjoyed being the follower, especially in this new land, with someone like Axel as a "playmate."

Then, as she began to untie her apron, Hanna said, "Lena, the postman left a postcard addressed to your name." She pulled the card out of her apron pocket and handed it to me.

For me? I was surprised. I could not believe that anyone knew where I was.

I stared at my name and the address scrawled on the outside of the card. It was from Peter. Yes, I remembered now that I had given him the address when we thought we might be taking the train together to Sweden and he was going to help me purchase my tickets.

"Come, come, let's hurry now. You can read the card later, Lena. Let's go to town and make sure that you can find some gifts for your friend, Michelle, and what was his name, that new beau of yours?"

I giggled. "Well, he's not exactly my beau, but a man I have gone out with only a few times. His name is Joseph."

"Well, it would be nice to bring him something from Sweden, wouldn't it?"

I slipped the postcard from Peter into my jeans pocket, to read later, and began to take off my hat and warm sweater, damp from the forest moisture. I could see that Hanna had laid out some food for Axel and me.

"I've set out a few things, some bratwurst, bread, cheese, and fruit for you both to eat before we leave. Now go ahead and wash up and eat quickly." I could tell Hanna had no problem bossing Axel around or anyone else. She did remind me a bit of Grandmother.

Soon we were on our way to Ronneby. I loved the small shops; a big park where a waterfall, not yet frozen, flowed from giant rocks; and the school children, in their Scandinavian-designed sweaters, mittens, and hats, carrying their bookbags from school, walking through the streets with laughter. They reminded me of when I was a child, though much less gregarious than these Swedish children.

Hanna suggested we go to a special shop of Swedish souvenirs, all with the blue-and-yellow flag on them. I never did much like these kinds of tourist items—we had plenty of those even in Astoria now—but I did not want to argue with this strong, opinionated woman.

It turned out well. I found a cute hat with the Swedish flag, small enough not to be garish, on the turned-up brim, which I thought Michelle would like to wear on cold days in Paris. For Joseph—well, it was harder to select just the right thing for him—finally, I settled on a small packet of lovely watercolors of Swedish landscapes. Of course, their cellophane packaging had a sticker in the shape of the Swedish flag, blue with yellow-crossed lines. I knew Joseph loved art as much as I did, maybe more, since he had grown up around his father's art gallery.

"Well, Lena, are you done?" asked Hanna. "Looks like you have some good choices. Now let's get home so I can prepare those mushrooms for dinner tonight." She bustled out the door of the shop and headed straight for her blue, slightly dented Volvo (I could imagine her having lots of fender-benders with the erratic way she drove). Axel and I held hands and followed like her two well-behaved offspring.

When we arrived home, Hanna went to the kitchen

to prepare dinner, Axel went outside to take care of the goats and chickens, and I went to my room, anxious to read Peter's postcard and to write Joseph.

Dear Lena,

After two great days skiing, I decided to come back to Sweden as my family was really upset with me and anxious to see me. I have a friend in Lund, so decided to stop there for a night to visit him before going on to Stockholm. You told me your family lives on a farm near Ronneby. I will be going that way and hope that I can see you. Please call me. -Peter

Though I was thrilled to hear from Peter and happy he wanted to see me, at the same time, I was anxious about taking time away from my detective work. I asked Hanna if she would mind if a friend came for a day and she replied not at all. She showed me how to use the phone, and after a few rings, Peter answered.

"*Hej*, Lena. Good to hear from you. I'm glad you received my postcard. Is it OK if I come by your family's place for a quick visit before heading north to Stockholm? I hope everything is going well for you and you're uncovering some of the mysteries you hoped to solve."

"Well, yes, Peter. It's slow, but I'm learning some details I never knew. Hanna—well, I mean my great aunt, wife of my uncle Johann—says it's fine if you want to come for a day. It will be fun to see you." Then, hesitating, I added, "I guess I should tell you I arrived too late. My uncle Johann died before my arrival."

There was silence on the other end of the telephone

connection, and then Peter said, "Wow, gee, Lena, I'm so sorry to hear that. My sympathies."

"Well, it was hard to learn that at first, but I am uncovering some things which I'll share with you when you arrive."

I proceeded to make plans to meet Peter at the train when he arrived the next day. Hanna offered to take me to the station. I had a mixture of excitement at seeing him and some trepidation. Could Peter help me? Or was he just going to be an interruption in my search for the secrets of Grandmother's past?

Chapter 23

Restless and unable to sleep that night, I circled my room in the old Swedish house, this house where my grandmother had lived as a young girl, before she immigrated to America. The walls of the room seemed to echo with her voice, a voice of sadness and despair. This was the same room where my mother, Sofia, as a small child stayed with her, in 1939. If only these walls could speak to me, I thought; if only they could tell me what happened that night Hanna said Johann came in late, distressed, and anxious—was that the word Hanna used to describe Johann those couple of days before Helga left Sweden for good, and earlier than expected?

Why was Johann anxious, and why did Axel want to show me Rebecca's and Johann's gravesites? Why also the Viking burial ground? Why did Axel lie down there in obvious emotional pain? He had said *far*, the Swedish word for father. How could it be that his father was buried there at that sacred site and why? How did he die? As a hero of the war? Axel had been a young child, maybe only six, when Helga said his father went off to the war. Would he have witnessed something? Surely losing his father at six years old must have been hard for him to understand. Axel seemed to think his father died—or was killed—and was buried there, but that didn't fit the other story I heard from Grandmother, that Gunnar had left the country to fight in the war in Germany and never came back. Did Gunnar defect? Choose Germany over his own country? So many questions screamed out in my mind.

· · ·

The following morning, having slept little, I wearily descended the steps to find Hanna and Axel seated at the kitchen table peeling apples. The smell of coffee had drifted up the stairs, and I longed for a cup now, to help waken me from my drowsiness after my almost sleepless night.

"God morgon," I said to Hanna and Axel, whose back was turned toward the kitchen door. Startled, he jumped up and clapped like a child, smiling at me, and offered his chair, with a gallant sweep of his hand motioning me to sit down. Hanna, too, stood up, wiped her apple-stained hands on her apron, walked to the cupboard above the sink, and reached for a cup.

"Well, God morgon to you, Lena. Your Swedish is improving. Axel and I were just commenting how late you must have slept."

Embarrassed, I glanced at my watch and realized that I had indeed slept late—finally, after several hours of walking around my room and writing in my journal, going over and over the questions that rolled in my head like dice, not knowing on which side they would land. Would there be an answer to the mystery I hoped to solve of why my grandmother screamed and took her own life?

"Well, yes, I guess I did finally fall asleep, close to morning, and slept longer than normal," I said. "Um, the coffee smells good."

"Ya, now come sit down and have some. Axel and I will fix you some breakfast." She smiled. "But with no herring."

We laughed.

Hanna poured me some coffee and set out a bowl of my favorite porridge. "Don't we have to pick up your friend soon—Peter? I think you said that was his name."

"Oh, yes, I almost forgot. I'll hurry and eat. His train from Lund is due at one o'clock. Do I have time to eat, Hanna?"

"Ya, no problem. I have to make the pie and then we'll leave in time to get to the station."

Axel was busy at the kitchen counter slicing thick pieces of pumpernickel bread for me. Hanna brought some butter and a bowl of fresh lingonberries to the table.

"Oh, I didn't mean to interrupt your apple-peeling. What are you preparing? I loved apples and couldn't help but feel homesick at the sweet-sour smell of the freshly peeled and sliced fruit. I remembered the apple dumplings Grandmother used to make.

"Well, what else but apple pie—you Americans are not the only ones to like apple pie, but we Swedes make it a bit differently than you do in America. I thought we could offer a piece of pie when your friend comes to-day; you know it is our custom to have kaffe and kakor in the afternoon."

"Ya, that would be nice," I replied.

I smiled, remembering how often Grandmother made the Swedish version of apple pie, no crust over the apples, but lots of sugar, butter, and flour mixed and poured over the top.

"The last of the apples from the old tree out front were about to go bad in the cold storage—it was time to put them to good use," said Hanna. "Come on, Axel, don't give up now. Help me finish pealing these apples while Lena eats her breakfast." Axel seemed good at interpreting Hanna's vivid gestures and simple Swedish orders.

While I drank my coffee and ate the bread with lingonberry jam, I mused about how often Grandmother and I had talked about Sweden around the kitchen table in Astoria. The memories prompted me to look up now from my plate and ask Hanna about the incident I experienced the day before with Axel. I hesitated, not sure if I should ask now or wait until Axel went out. Perhaps mention of Gunnar would be painful for him— I flashed back to the memory of the tears in his eyes when he lay down on the ground at the Viking site.

Instead of bringing up Gunnar directly, I cleared my throat and said, "Hanna, I hope you have remembered more from the past you can share with me. For instance, some things about my grandmother's other brother, not Johann."

Axel looked up from his apple pealing, stared at me bewildered and then rose abruptly and left the kitchen. Maybe he did understand some English. It was hard to understand what this prescient man understood and didn't.

"Oh, don't pay attention to him," Hanna said. "He gets in a mood whenever his father is brought up. I guess it's normal given his father left him with us—I mean with Johann and me—to raise. Sad for him."

"I do have to admit, that is sad for me to think about, too," I said, "since I lost my father when I was still an infant, younger than Axel was. Of course, I don't remember a thing about him. All I know was he was lost at sea in a fishing-boat accident."

"Ya, Johann told me about that. Your grandmother wrote Johann about the accident, and said she was going to move in with your mother and you to help."

"Yes, that's right," I said. "That's when we heard her call out often at night in her sleep. As I've already mentioned, Mother always felt that her screams had something to do with what happened here in Sweden during her visit."

Hanna looked down at her lap, laid down her paring knife, got up abruptly and walked to the sink, where she stared out the window, like she did a few days before when she and I discussed the past. It was as if the mention of that night hung like a dark shroud over her memories, ones she wished to forget.

Hanna's slumped shoulders straightened, and she appeared to be composing herself. She turned from the window and looked right at me. "Ya, I think perhaps your mother was right, Lena. Those were hard times with the sudden death of Rebecca and then all that was going on in Europe, so close to us, and Gunnar threatening to go to Germany to help fight the war."

"What?" I looked up at Hannah. "What do you mean, Gunnar going off to help fight the war in Germany— do you mean he wanted to help Hitler?" I didn't want to let Hanna know what Mrs. Lundberg had told me for fear Hanna would clam up again. I needed more information.

Hanna sucked in her breath as if to take a moment to compose herself, to have some time before answering my question. She looked back out the window, then turned and walked slowly back to the kitchen table, sat down, letting out a sigh, and said, "Well, ya, Lena, you're right—it was awful for Johann to learn his brother had joined a group of young Nazis here in Sweden, those who supported Hitler's desire to conquer all of Europe and create the pure Aryan race, by getting rid of those who, well, were like Rebecca."

As I listened to Hanna, my hands began to sweat; I felt the blood drain from my face with this revelation. Grandmother had never mentioned anything like this, but now it started to become clearer, why she never wanted to talk about Gunnar, the somber young man who stood slightly behind her in the photograph with Johann and Rebecca at her side. It wasn't just because he once tried to do something terrible to her in the Blekinje woods just before she immigrated—it was more that she learned he was a Nazi sympathizer. I wondered if Axel knew this about his father—but, of course, probably not. He had been only a small boy. How could he have known or even understood? Suddenly it all made sense. I remembered once Grandmother mentioning that Johann changed Axel's given name from Adolf to Axel. Gunnar had named his son Adolf, after his hero, of course.

A cloud of silence hung over the kitchen, the only sounds that of the coffee percolating on the stove and the scratching of a bird at the windowsill where Hanna had put out some apple seeds.

When I could find my voice again to speak, I asked Hanna, "Can you tell me any more about this?"

"Not a lot, Lena, but I do remember what disturbed Johann the most were the nights that Gunnar left the house and went to the village where he met Axel's mother— Johann suspected, the same village where he met with the Nazi group."

"Can you tell me how to get to that village, Hanna?" I asked, knowing that might be the next place I would have to search for clues. "What was the name of Gunnar's wife, her family name? I would really like to meet them. Maybe they could shed more light on why my grandmother had such dark memories."

"Well, Lena, maybe it's best you leave the past in the past," Hanna said. "What good will it do to know more now? Your grandmother is gone, and you're young and have your whole future ahead of you."

"Hanna, you don't seem to understand why this is so important for me." I leaned toward her over the table and, in frustration, lightly pounded my fist on it. With as serious a tone of voice as I could muster, I said, "I have a severe difficulty sleeping at nights, I suspect from the memories of my grandmother's screams. Maybe if I learn why she did that I can find some peace—the peace she never did find. Her memories haunted her so much that she walked into the ocean and took her own life. Do you really understand that?"

Hanna made a slight adjustment in her seat, leaning back some, and looked down at her lap and sighed, as if resigned to listening to my imploring voice. "Yes, I remember the tears in Johann's eyes when he read the letter from your mother—that I do," she said.

"Please, Hanna, now that Uncle Johann has died, you—and maybe Axel—are my only connection to the past. Please," I implored again, "tell me everything you know and can remember."

As if finally resigned to answering my pleas, Hanna stood up again, picked up the silver coffee pot, poured another cup for me and one for herself, sat back down, and said, "Lena, I can't remember the name of Axel's mother, at least the first name, but the family name was Furugârd—yes, that's it, Furugârd. The father was a shopkeeper. I don't remember what they sold, maybe paper goods. I don't remember. He was apparently the leader of the Nazi group—there were many followers in that town. I can take you there if you think you must find them. But we must be careful to not let Axel know we're going there. He thinks his mother is dead—and maybe she is. He would not understand why we are digging up the past—partly his past, too."

"Oh, tack, Hanna," I said, almost wanting to hug her, but holding myself back, not knowing if this would bother her. Her reserve suggested she would not feel comfortable with effusive hugs. "Can we go today, please?"

Hanna appeared agitated for a moment and then looked up at me with a smile that looked pasted-on to her countenance. "No, not today—remember your friend is coming this afternoon."

"Oh, yes." Embarrassed, I admitted, for a moment, I'd almost forgotten about Peter's expected visit.

"But," Hanna went on, "maybe tomorrow. I don't like to leave Axel here completely on his own. He sometimes suffers deep depression and I worry about him—what he might do. I have to ask Mrs. Neilson, our neighbor, to come over and be here with him. Axel likes her very much."

"That's fine, Hanna." I realized it would not do any good to push her further for answers to my questions. Besides, I needed time to plan what I would ask if we found relatives of Axel's in the town we were to visit. Maybe Peter would have some ideas. In fact, I thought, maybe he could shed more light on the existence of Nazi sympathizers in Sweden. Perhaps he had learned about that in his schooling or from his family. Maybe this was an ideal time for his visit. I began to look forward to seeing him.

Hanna had retreated to the back porch to give Axel the bag of apple peelings to take out to the goats.

"Oh, and what did you say the name of the village is, Hanna?" I called out to her.

"Småstad, Lena." Hanna walked back into the kitchen. "It's about seventy kilometers from here, maybe an hour of time. We'll try to go tomorrow around ten in the morning, but now you better finish eating and do whatever you have to upstairs while I make the pie, before we leave for the train station."

"Oh, yes, of course. Tack, Hanna. I have to finish a letter to Joseph. I'd like to mail it in town, if that's not a problem. Then I'll change, comb my hair, and put on my nicer sweater. I do want to look nice for Peter."

Hanna smiled and raised a curious eyebrow. "Well, another boyfriend, hah, Lena? You mentioned Joseph before."

"Oh, no, Peter's not a boyfriend at all, just a nice friend I met at the Sorbonne in Paris. Since he's Swedish, I enjoyed talking with him about my heritage, and he helped me figure out the way I would come here by the train. I'll leave you to your apple pie now. As I said, I have a few things to do upstairs. Just call for me, please, when it's time to leave."

Hanna looked relieved, maybe glad to avoid any more of my persistent questions. "Fine, Lena. We'll go into town about twelve-thirty to meet your friend when he arrives at the Ronneby station. I'll make the pie while you go upstairs now," Hanna said. "We'll talk more later."

Chapter 24

As soon as I got back to my room, I pulled my bathrobe on over my clothes and wrapped myself in its softness, grabbed my fountain pen and an aerogram:

Dear Joseph,

I'm finally getting somewhere in my search for the answers to why Grandmother screamed.

I miss Paris and, of course, you. I hope we can get together when I return and begin again.

I remember our last date when you played the piano for me, Chopin, I think. It was lovely.

I hope you will play again. I'm not having any time to sketch while I'm here, too busy trying to uncover the secrets of the past, which haunted my grandmother. I have seen some charming artwork in a local shop. Well, à bientôt. I think of you every day! ~Lena

P.S. Say bonjour to Dr. Lanier

I set my pen down and wondered if that was too

intimate to write to Joseph. We'd had only a few dates before I'd had to leave Paris, but we had kissed, and he'd called me "chérie." Well, I will see if he responds, I thought to myself. I hoped he would like the gift I bought him.

I mused a moment about my talks with Hanna and then picked up my pen again and opened my journal to record the details of my discoveries so far:

"I'm finally getting somewhere in my search for the answers to why Grandmother screamed. Hanna, against her will, I think, revealed a dark secret—one that shocked me—but now is maybe making some sense. Great-Uncle Gunnar, Grandmother's brother, was a Nazi. He used to meet with other Swedish Nazi sympathizers, supportive of Hitler's agenda to exterminate all Jews. I can hardly believe this horror, but Hanna says it's true and that is why Johann maybe adopted Axel, whose real name was Adolf, when he was little, when Hanna says Gunnar ran off to join Hitler's armies. I somehow doubt this. I'm looking forward to visiting the village where Axel's mother lived. She may still be alive. Probably in her sixties, which isn't unrealistic to think. These Swedes are hearty souls, I've observed. I will try to find someone in town who can tell me more. I sense I'm getting close to something—something important.

If I can find the answers, maybe I'll surprise Joseph and return to Paris sooner than I thought, soon enough to celebrate the New Year. I'm sad I won't be there for Noël, which is just in a week, but this is so important, I cannot give up now on my search to learn the truth. I must remember to talk to Peter about when he's returning to Paris—maybe we can travel on the train together.

All will depend on what I find out in the next few days."

I loved the scratchy sound my fountain pen made across my journal pages; it made me feel I was getting somewhere in my search for the truth. I glanced at my watch and realized that Hanna would soon be waiting for me to leave for the train station.

As I was preparing to leave my room, I heard a noise from somewhere upstairs—maybe from an attic. I had noticed a door that was always closed down the hallway and next to a room Hanna had indicated was Johann's old room. I wanted to look around but didn't dare. Perhaps it would be inappropriate to trespass so soon after his death. I didn't want to be nosey, so hadn't asked Hanna where the other door led. Now, as I was exiting my room, the door next to Johann's opened, and Hanna stepped out, quickly closing and locking the door behind her. I had just enough time to glimpse a stairway behind her. Where did it lead? An attic, most likely, or another bedroom? I didn't ask.

Hanna seemed ruffled and flushed. "Oh, you're ready, Lena. Gut." She brushed past me and ran quickly down the stairs and towards the mud porch.

"Come now, we must go," she said, glancing back at me.

All I could think about was what lay behind that locked door, where the stairs led? Why did Hanna seem like she was hiding something? More questions rolled around in my head. I followed Hanna downstairs, grabbed my jacket and put on my boots, then ran out the door. Hanna had already started the Volvo's motor. Axel was in the back seat, and I settled into the front passenger seat. Hanna took off.

Once we had turned onto the main road into

Ronneby, I finally took a deep breath and asked with some caution, "Hanna, I hope you won't think me too curious, but what's upstairs behind that door you locked?"

"Oh, Lena, you do ask a lot of questions."

Memories of times Grandmother had said the same words came to my mind.

There was a long pause, and then Hanna continued, "Well, if you really need to know, I was upstairs in the attic just to find some old things I store there." That's funny, I thought. She didn't have anything in her hands except the door key when she emerged. "Nothing you need to know about—at least for now."

"Why did Hanna add "at least for now?"

She seemed anxious to change the subject.

"While you were upstairs, I made the pie and also prepared the muchrooms you and Axel gathered to go with our meatballs tonight," said Hanna. "Do you think your friend will be staying for dinner?"

"Oh, I'm not sure. He didn't say. I think he's going on to Stockholm to be with his family for the holiday."

"Gut, well, we can ask him when he arrives. Tonight, after we eat, I'll show you more of Johann's photos and share something I know you will like."

Now I was even more curious, and anxious to see the photos and the mysterious surprise Hanna had implied was in store for me.

Chapter 25

When we pulled into the Ronneby station, it was crowded. Hanna had a hard time finding parking, so I encouraged her to let me out and just remain with the car near the exit. She agreed, and I headed for the station as the train pulled in. I was beginning to feel like a celebrity in Ronneby. Every time I came to the station, there were newsmen around with cameras and a milling crowd. I later learned from Hanna that it was due to the controversial far-right politician who just happened to be campaigning at the time and had many followers in Ronneby. I knew little about the politics of Sweden and was preoccupied now with meeting Peter. Just as I reached the station platform, I saw him step off the train with his backpack and that cute black captain's hat he'd worn the day I first met him at the Shakespeare and Co. bookstore. I called out his name and he came towards me with his long stride and a big smile. He gave me a quick peck on the cheek, which I wasn't prepared for. I blushed and realized how glad I was to see him again.

"Wow, Lena, you fit in perfectly here—a real *Svenska flicka!*"

I'm sure I turned three more shades of red, looked down a moment, and then caught my breath and said, "Well, tack, Peter, I must admit, it's wonderful learning about my grandmother's country and meeting a couple of my relatives—well, almost relatives. Before we go over to the car where my uncle's second wife, Hanna, is waiting for us, I must explain a couple of things."

Peter slipped his arm in mine and said, "Sure, Lena, tell me what I should know."

I hesitated for a moment, not quite knowing how to start. "Well, for starters you're not only going to meet Hanna, who I guess is my aunt by marriage, but you're also going to meet my second cousin, Axel. He's probably about forty-something, but in many ways seems like a young teen. He was born with an undiagnosed, that I know of, brain condition, so does not speak much, but amazingly seems to understand much, and besides, he's dear and kind and I'm growing very fond of him. Secondly, as you know, I was trying to learn about my grandmother's experiences when she visited here in 1939—what might have taken place that made her scream in her sleep and ultimately take her own life. I was hoping to talk with her brother, Johann, but, as I told you on the phone, he died two weeks before I arrived."

"Ya, Lena, I was sorry to hear that. Well, has Hanna been able to answer some of your questions?" said Peter.

I ignored his question and just said, "Come on, Peter, we better head to the car. I can see Hanna waving now from where she parked. I'll finish the rest of the story later." Peter and I made our way in, out, and around the many parked cars and finally arrived at the old blue Volvo.

"Välkommen, Peter. We're glad you could come and visit Lena and us, too." Hanna nodded towards Axel, who looked down shyly. "She's told us a lot about you."

Peter looked as surprised as I felt. "She has?" he said and looked at me with a pleased smile.

"Well, not really," I said, wondering why Hanna had said that. "After all, I don't know you that well yet. All I said to Hanna was that you helped me plan my trip here to Sweden."

Hanna motioned to me to jump in the back with Axel and for Peter to get in the front passenger seat next to her. "Come now, we can all talk when we get back to the house."

Once on the road, and after an awkward silence, I spoke up and said to Peter, "I'd like to introduce you to Axel." Peter turned in his seat and looked back at Axel, who sat behind Hanna.

Axel tipped his hat and nodded with a big smile to Peter, who in kind tipped his hat. I knew the two would get on well immediately.

Peter helped fill the awkward silences with tales of his recent ski trip to Chamonix, his knee injury from a fall, which I could tell embarrassed him to admit but explained the slight limp I had noticed he had at the train station.

"So," Peter said, "I decided it was time for me to bag the skiing and head for Stockholm where my family seemed anxious to have me home for the Yuletide festivities. I have a boyhood friend who is going to the university in Lund, and he wanted me to stop there to see him before continuing on to Stockholm. We had a great time for a couple of days, and now I'm happy to be here—admit I've never seen this part of Skåne." Peter looked out the window and said, "Looks pretty rural and nice."

"Ya, it is. We're small-town folk and like our space and privacy," said Hanna. "Can't quite imagine living in the big city where you're from, Peter. I've only been to Stockholm once, when I was a teen, and I was glad to get back here to our farm and Blekinge woods."

Peter turned to look back at me. "How about you, Lena? This is quite a change from Paris. How are you liking it here?"

Feeling a bit like a trapped rabbit, I said, "Well, Peter, I have to admit I love Paris, but it's been a real pleasure to meet Hanna and Axel and to be on their beautiful property, the farm. Wait until you see it. There are fields of potatoes, goats and chickens, and very near is a hill with an ancient Viking burial ground marked by huge stones with runes."

"Well, that's very interesting. I have an older brother who has been studying our Viking relatives for a long time. He'd be fascinated to see that."

"Ya, and the woods are not far away. Axel has taught Lena how to find the mushrooms that are safe to eat this time of year. Of course, it's almost impossible to find chanterelles this season. Are you staying for dinner tonight, Peter?" asked Hanna.

"Gosh, I'd like to, but my family is expecting me. I'm afraid I'm going to have to ask you to take me back to the train station at five to catch the five-thirty train," said Peter.

"Oh, I'm happy to take you back, Peter, but I'm

sure Lena will be disappointed you can't stay longer," Hanna offered, with a nod and a smile towards me.

I squirmed in my seat, feeling in a tight spot, not sure what to say. On one hand, I knew I would enjoy Peter's company, but my focus was really on getting to the bottom of what happened here in 1939. I saw Peter as a distraction. Just as I was trying to think of what to say next, Hanna swerved into the lane that led to the house and Peter filled the silence.

"Wow, this is really beautiful. I love the trees and the forest we just passed. I'm hoping to study forest management and environmental science. I guess I will have to get over being a city guy and spend more time in the woodlands of Sweden."

"That you will have to do, Peter. We have plenty of open space and woodlands here, we do," said Hanna as she pulled up in front of the house. "Now gather up your things, Lena, Axel, and Peter, and come in for some kaffe y kakor."

"Thank you, I'd like to walk around your land a bit first with Lena, if that's OK, Hanna," said Peter.

Axel jumped out and came around and opened the door for me as Peter and Hanna got out of the car in the front.

"Oh, of course, do what you two would like, and when you're ready, come in for coffee. *Det är bra!*" said Hanna.

Hanna found it no trouble slipping from English to Swedish and back again, something Johann must have taught her.

With a smile and a glance towards me, Peter said, "Well then, *c'est bon!*"

I laughed. "Oh, Hanna and Axel, Peter is just

showing off his French now."

They laughed and Hanna turned to Axel and said in Swedish, "Come on in the house with me. Let Lena and Peter have some time together to explore."

With a crestfallen look on his face, Axel picked up Peter's backpack and headed up the front steps with Hanna.

"Gee, thanks, Axel, for taking my backpack in!" said Peter in Swedish.

Axel turned and waved back at Peter with a big grin on his face. I was happy the two could slip easily into a friendly relationship.

As the front door to the mud room closed, Peter took my arm and said, "Well, Lena, show me around and tell me what you're looking for. Maybe I can help."

I proceeded to give Peter a few of the details I already had uncovered. I explained that there were still gaps in Hanna's story, like what did she see out the window; where did the scream she witnessed all those years ago come from during my grandmother's visit; what happened to Axel's father, my grandmother's brother Gunnar? Why did he suddenly disappear and leave his six-year-old son in the care of Johann, and, of course, how did Rebecca, Johann's Jewish wife, die so suddenly, though I really was convinced it was from poisoning.

Peter was intrigued and began immediately to act like a natural detective. "Well, it looks like, for one thing, you are right, Lena—a visit to the village where Gunnar often went to visit his wife, or maybe not wife, but mother of his son, Axel, is a good place to start. As far as the scream Hanna heard one morning—did she say that your grandmother decided to go back to

America right after that, earlier than planned? I wonder why? Something must have happened to cause her concern or fear. That could be connected to the scream Hanna heard."

"That's what I think too," I said. "Hanna saw something out the kitchen window and said that Johann and my grandmother didn't act normal after that or seemed in distress."

"Have you looked out that same window, Lena?"

"Well, to tell you the truth, I haven't. That's a good idea."

"Come on, we can go around the house and see what we can see. You must be able to identify where the kitchen is."

"Oh, yes, I can. Axel and I came in from collecting mushrooms through the back door, right off the kitchen the other day and—" Before I could finish my sentence, Peter grabbed my hand and began walking to the back of the house.

"Come on, let's see what's there."

As we rounded the side and approached the back steps, I looked to the right and said, "Oh, Peter, look, there's a shed there next to that big field. Hanna said that's where they plant their crop of potatoes and sugar beets every year, two of their cash crops."

"Yea, that makes sense, Lena. The people in this area of Sweden are mostly farmers. We Swedes call this the 'grain basket' of Sweden."

"I wonder what they use the shed for?" I pondered. "Probably their farm tools, wouldn't you think? Or maybe that's where they make the goats cheese."

"Ya, I suppose you're right. Did you look around it or go in?" Peter asked.

"No, I didn't," I said. I looked back to the kitchen window and tried to see if I could see Hanna looking out at us, but no, she didn't appear to be at the window.

"Let's try the door, Peter."

"Ya, let's!" he said.

We soon discovered the door was locked. There were two small, very dirty windows that we peered through, but could not make out much that was in the shed—maybe some tools, and there was a big wood table in the middle with some large pots, spoons, boxes of something we couldn't identify.

"Come on, Lena, let's go around to the other side. Looks like there's a back window too. With the light coming in from the west now, we might be able to see better there." Peter ran around ahead of me, and as I came up to him, he looked up with a quizzical expression.

"So, what do you make of this, Lena? Any Nazis in the family?"

I gasped as I looked where he was pointing. Into the windowsill was carved, as with a pocketknife, a perfect swastika with the initials GP next to it.

"Oh, yes, I didn't mention that, Peter. Gunnar was evidently involved in a group of Nazi sympathizers just before the war. Hitler was a kind of idol for them, I think."

"Whoa—you mean you had family members who supported the Nazi regime in Germany?"

"Well, no, I don't think there was anyone else in the family; in fact, I believe that Johann and his sister, my grandmother, were quite upset when they learned about that, but I don't have all the facts, and Hanna doesn't seem to know much about that. She keeps saying that

Gunnar went off to the war but supplies little more information other than that Axel was Gunnar's son, and Johann and she were committed to taking care of him. I hope to learn more about that when I visit the village where Gunnar often went—how that may connect with my grandmother's screams and fears after her visit here I do not know yet."

"Lena, Peter." Hanna was calling us from the back door. "Come in for coffee now."

I had little time to talk to Peter more or to think about the events of 1939, as Hanna insisted on playing the good hostess. She had set out a beautiful tray of cookies and apple pie with coffee for us in the dining room, where the table was decorated with a Yule wreath of holly and pine boughs and a delightful tomte, the Christmas gnome, carved from wood.

Peter seemed impressed with it and asked about the carver.

"Oh, that was Johann. He could make anything, carved all the time when he wasn't practicing his violin." She looked off, into where we could not tell, but I was sure she was missing the one man she loved in her life, perhaps besides Axel.

It was soon time to leave again to take Peter to the train station. We all went out to the car, and this time Axel got in front with Hanna. It appeared they had pre-planned this. Peter and I were in the back.

We tossed back and forth, hitting shoulders and knees as Hanna rode over the bumpy road to get to the main highway. Peter laughed and I smiled and began to relax in the company of this easygoing Swede, with blue eyes like mine and an expression that still reminded me of my father, the only memory I had of him, the photo my mother had given me for my locket. I began to regret Peter had to leave so soon.

Once at the station, Peter leaned down before jumping up into the train and gave me a quick peck on the cheek. Again, I didn't know how to react but just laughed and thanked him for coming. In the car we had discussed returning to Paris together if I managed to get all the answers I sought by that time. Peter gave me his phone number at his family's house, and we wished each other a *God Jul*—Merry Christmas. The train pulled out of the station, and I could see Peter waving at me from a window as it chugged north towards Stockholm.

He hadn't been able to help me find the answers I sought, but he had confirmed Gunnar was indeed a Nazi sympathizer and that maybe the red shed played some kind of role in what Hanna had seen out the window when she heard the scream. I still had more questions than answers.

Hanna, Axel, and I were quiet going back to the house. Once inside I told Hanna I needed to rest, and she agreed we'd talk more over dinner later.

Chapter 26

That night, after we had eaten, Hanna, Axel, and I went to the living room. It was a rather dark-ish room with a huge old oriental carpet, dark wood-stained walls, an overstuffed settee, crocheted doilies on the arms. Artwork of numerous Swedish artists, like Carl Larsson and others whose names I didn't know, adorned the wall. Carved wooden candlesticks sat on ta-bles here and there. Hanna explained that Johann had made the candlesticks. Some were painted in Swedish colors of blue and yellow, others left in natural wood, all with lit candles in them. The soft candlelight lent a cozy feeling to the room. Hanna motioned for me to sit on the big settee with her. Axel lowered his bulky body down into one of the big overstuffed armchairs. There was a fire in the fireplace that Axel had prepared with wood before our meal. The coals glowed a bright red in the dimly lit room and added the warmth I craved.

Several what appeared to be photo albums sat on a coffee table in front of the settee. Hanna picked up one of the dark-colored leather albums, much like the one I remembered Grandmother had. She motioned for me to sit closer as she opened the album and began to explain some of the photos. "This couple are your great-grandparents." The couple was standing in front of the blacksmith shop I recognized as the same that Grandmother had shown me. They stared straight at the camera and looked grim and stern.

"Well, they certainly don't look very happy," I commented.

"Times were hard then, Lena," Hanna offered in defense of the old couple. "My parents were poor, too. We lived a short distance from the Peterssons and were their closest neighbors. I used to play with Johann, you know, when we were growing up. By high school he had become a very handsome man, and I had a hankering for him. Ya, I wanted him to be my beau. Your grandmother, Helga, didn't seem to like me much, and besides, she was always reading when she wasn't helping her mother. She left about that time for America and Johann got deeper into his music and violin-playing. Soon after that, we were all hit with the Spanish flu, the 1918 pandemic. Your great-grandparents became very ill and died. Johann and Gunnar had to take care of all the duties of the farm. I didn't see much of them for a few years."

"Oh, go on Hanna. This is all very interesting. I like hearing these details that Grandmother Helga never shared with me." I was anxious to get to the parts about Helga's visit, and Gunnar and Rebecca.

"Well, then, I heard Johann had gone off on a scholarship from Lund University to study music in Prague. The next thing you know, seven or eight years later, he returned with a wife from Poland, Rebecca. The two of them performed all over Europe but lived mostly near Rebecca's family in Warsaw. Johann said he loved his life in Poland, performing with Rebecca, who was also a violinist. Adolf Hitler was threatening the Jews, and Rebecca's family urged the couple to leave and be safe in Sweden. If I remember correctly, they had already sent Rebecca's younger sister to Denmark on a ship with lots of other Jewish children to keep them from the evil hands of the Nazis. I think Rebecca wanted to come here to try and search for her sister. Johann wanted the best for Rebecca, most of all her safety. He called me to come and be their maid. I needed the work, as I was helping my aging parents. I was the only one of my siblings by then who hadn't immigrated to America."

Hanna paused for a minute—there were tears in her eyes. She dabbed at them with a white cotton hanky she pulled from her apron pocket, sighed, and looked into my eyes. Finally, she said, "I admit, I still loved your great-uncle Johann, Lena."

I didn't know what to say to Hanna, somewhat aghast at this admission—Hanna loved my uncle from the time she was a young girl? I reached my hand out to touch her arm lightly, and said, "I understand," but I really didn't.

Hanna sucked in her breath and continued, "Well, there isn't much more to add. I worked hard as a maid. Rebecca was very particular about how I should do things, fussy, I would say, but I know she tried to be kind, too. She was so much more worldly than me, having played the violin in concerts all over Europe. She and Johann were very talented musicians, you know." Her voice trailed off.

"Yes, I remember Grandmother telling me that," I said, "but I never fully understood how Rebecca died. Grandmother would never talk about it—only suggested it happened when she visited in the Spring of 1939."

Hanna nodded and said, "When they came back here, Rebecca was sad, as she had to say good-bye to her family in Warsaw. It wasn't long after that she received word of their being swept up by the Nazis and sent to the ghettos there. Johann tried to shake her out of her depression, but she was almost inconsolable. They would often take trips on the weekends to Stockholm and other places in the North to see if they could find out information about the Jewish children who had been adopted by Swedish families, hoping they would find Rebecca's sister. She was always worried and sad. That's probably why she couldn't get pregnant. They wanted a baby desperately. Johann confided his frustration with me, but I couldn't do anything. I was the housekeeper, you know—the poor neighbor girl."

I noted a tone of bitterness in Hanna's voice, or was it martyrdom?

Hanna continued, "Your grandmother and mother brought much-needed sunshine into the house when they came to visit. Rebecca and Helga had an immediate liking for one another."

Hanna turned the page of the album and seemed to want to change the subject. "Well, let's go on. Here's a photo taken of Johann, Rebecca, and your grandmother holding little Sofia."

"Oh, it's almost the same as the one Grandmother showed me," I said.

Axel stood up, and though he had been very quiet to this point, he seemed interested in the photo of him handing flowers to my mother when she was a small girl. He let out enthusiastic grunts as he pointed a finger to himself in the photo and laughed.

"Axel, why don't you go and get more wood for the fire," Hanna said. "You've seen these photos a hundred times. Go now. We'll have our tea and kakor soon."

I sensed there was something Hanna was about to show me that she did not wish for Axel to see.

Shoulders slumped in resignation, Axel went out to the hallway, donned his woolen hat and his bulky down jacket, and went out the door.

"There now," Hanna said. "I can show you a couple of photos that I don't like to have Axel see, as he gets so depressed."

She proceeded to slide her hand across the photo as if to erase a memory. Then, with her chubby index finger, she tapped the photo of a stern-looking, tow-headed man, hair cut very short, stockier in build than Johann, and said, "This is Gunnar, the younger of the brothers."

I looked down at the photo and recognized the sad, or was it angry, face of the man I had seen standing in the shadows in my photo, the one I had in my backpack, the one I had looked at a hundred times, wondering why he looked so angry. Suddenly, I could see, for the first time, a resemblance between him and Axel.

"Yes, Hanna," I said, "I have seen him in a photo Grandmother had. She would always close the album at that point and seemed not ever to want to talk about him, the other brother."

"Ya, I know. There was something dark between them. I hesitate to tell you this, Lena, but perhaps you deserve to know."

I shuddered to think there was going to be another revelation even worse than the facts I already knew, that Gunnar had been a part of the Swedish young Nazis. What worse could she reveal?

"Please go on, Hanna—you know I need all the information that might help me to understand Grandmother."

Hanna took a deep breath. "Well, Johann confided in me many years later, after we were married, of course, that your mother held a great fear and hatred of their younger brother—in fact Johann did, too. It was he who saved your mother from . . . it's hard to say—being *violated*, is that the word?—by her brother in the dark woods of Blekinge one day when they were walking home from school, just six months before your mother immigrated with her friend, Marta, to the United States."

I pretended to gasp in surprise, having already learned this from Mrs. Lundberg back in Astoria. Then I blurted out: "Do you mean raped?" I had to lead Hanna on, with hopes that she would reveal more—why Gunnar behaved the way he did toward his younger sister.

"Well, yes, I guess that is the word you use for it in English. Gunnar was always resentful of his sister, your grandmother, because their father seemed to favor her. He brought her books to read and stood up for her when the brothers taunted or teased her too much."

"Now I understand Grandmother's fury when I asked too many questions about him," I said.

"Ya, that was probably the reason, Lena. But now let's not talk of these dark things anymore. I have a surprise for you." She went to a small chest in the corner of the room, near the entrance to the hallway. She opened the door of the chest and drew out an old violin, much like the one that Grandmother had left me, with the note saying it had been Rebecca's.

"Oh, yes," I said, "this is almost like the one that Grandmother left for me the night she committed suicide. She said Johann had given it to her when she departed to return to America with my mother. I had always hoped to learn to play it, but with my studies and work, I never seemed to have the time. I remember Grandmother saying how beautifully Johann and Rebecca played duets for her before Rebecca died so unexpectedly."

"Ya, they could make beautiful music together, and Rebecca sang, too. Often Johann would play the violin and Rebecca would sing along. We would have concerts in the living room and Axel always loved those. He was, you know, very fond of Rebecca also. She gave him the mothering he seemed to miss. We never saw his mother. She lived in another village, the one we're going to visit tomorrow. Gunnar would bring Axel to stay with us. I was glad when Johann and Rebecca sometimes invited me to stay to listen to their music after working all day."

Hanna paused for a minute as if remembering those long-ago days. "Here, come look again at the photos I have of them playing together."

I pored over the photos for the next fifteen minutes or so while Hanna went to the kitchen to fetch something. She returned to the parlor with a tray with the silver coffee pot, cups and saucers, and a dish of small poppy-seed cakes and ginger cookies.

Axel came in with a big stack of wood in his arms,

his nose rosy from the cold outside. As soon as he saw the tray, he smiled widely, put down the wood, stoked the fire, and then joined us for coffee and kakor. The dark cloud that had hung over the room at the revelation of Gunnar's crime began to lift.

"Go ahead and play us a tune, Axel," said Hanna. "Show Lena what your uncle Johann taught you."

Axel picked up the violin and played a melancholy tune—was it Chopin? I recognized the woeful music from the time in Paris after my second date with Joseph when he played the piano for me at his family's home. Chopin was his favorite. I had a wave of longing for him as I listened to the music. I could understand now the love that Rebecca must have felt for Johann and him for her.

"No, no, Axel, play something happier to end our day with Lena," said Hanna.

Axel looked down, dejected, and then lifted the violin to his chin, and with his bow hand began to strike out a happy tune. Hanna said it was a Swedish folk song. His body swayed with the music and his eyes twinkled. Lost in thought, I tapped my feet to the beat of the music.

"There, that's it," said Hanna. She turned to me and said, "He's pretty good, isn't he? In spite of his mental incapacity."

I was thankful that Axel understood so little English. Then Hanna stood up and, as abruptly as she had asked Axel to play, said in Swedish, "That's enough for tonight, Axel. Lena has to get her night's rest before our drive tomorrow."

Axel lowered the violin from his chin, slipped it with the bow back into its case, and turned to go out of the room. He looked back at me with a warm smile and said, "God natt."

"God natt, Axel. And to you too, Hanna. Thank you for sharing the photos with me and more." I stopped myself, knowing that Axel was still within hearing range. I did not want to make him sad at the mention of his father's name. "I'll go up to bed now and see you both in the morning."

Chapter 27

When I arrived at the bottom of the stairs the next morning, I was greeted by a stranger. "Good morning. You must be Hanna's niece from Paris," the woman said as she extended her right hand.

Was that what Hanna had told this woman, that I was her niece? Well, I guessed that was partially true; after all, Uncle Johann married Hanna a few years after his wife, Rebecca, died. I had a vague recollection that Grandmother was not too happy when she received the announcement of Hanna and Johann's marriage.

"Um—yes." Usually feeling awkward with strangers, especially with those to whom I might have to reveal my poor Swedish, I hesitated. There were no sounds from the kitchen. I wondered where Hanna and Axel might have gone.

As if reading my mind, the woman said, "Hanna and Axel just stepped out to feed the chickens and goats. They'll be back in a minute. Why don't we have some coffee and get to know one another. I understand Hanna is going to take you for a ride around our neck of the woods, as we sometimes say here, to show you some of the local scenery."

I soon understood that this was the friend Hanna mentioned would stay with Axel while we went to the village where she thought that Gunnar's wife had lived. I could tell that the woman had no idea of my mission.

"Yes, that would be nice. I'm ready for coffee and maybe some of the good porridge Hanna makes."

I followed the woman down the hallway to the kitchen. Tall, with slightly greying hair pulled up in a bun, she wore practical wool tweed slacks, a bulky cream-colored sweater, and heavy leather boots, not at all the way Hanna dressed. There was nothing really distinctive about this woman, whose name I learned was Astrid, but she did seem kind.

Just as we sat down at the kitchen table with our coffee, Hanna came in and called out, "We're back." She hurried into the kitchen, slightly out of breath. "Well, Lena, good to see you're awake. As soon as you have some porridge and coffee, we'll leave. I see you and Astrid have met." The two women smiled amiably at one another. I had the impression that they probably shared secrets and maybe local gossip, too.

Axel trailed in behind Hanna and helped himself to coffee, nodding with a smile at me and Astrid.

An awkward silence followed while Hanna bustled about dishing up the porridge from a pot on the stove. She grabbed the lingonberry jam jar and a basket of *ebelskiver*s, which she offered Astrid and me.

"Oh, Hanna, no thank you. Just coffee for me. You know me. I ate early this morning before coming over here."

Axel left the room and returned with a checkerboard

and a bag of checkers, which he set down on the sideboard of the kitchen.

Hanna laughed. "Well, I guess I know what you two will be doing while we're gone," she said as she glanced at Axel, who was setting up the checkerboard and laying out the black and red round pieces.

Hanna and I finished our coffee, stood, and said our good-byes. It was a cold day, but the sun was bright.

"Be sure and bundle up, Lena," Hanna said. "It's bitter cold today. Br-r-r!"

We climbed into Hanna's old Volvo and drove off down the long country lane past the Blekinge woods and out onto the main road. A few cars passed, and Hanna waved at some of the passing drivers. I had the impression that this sparsely populated part of Sweden was one of friendly neighborhood farmers and tradespeople, one where everyone knew almost everyone else's business. Then again, that may not be true. I knew from experience, growing up in Astoria, that Swedes were reserved people, more prone to keep things to themselves.

I was nervous and fidgeted with the fringe on my long woolen neck scarf, anxious about what lay ahead in Smästad, the village where Gunnar used to meet with the Nazi group, according to Hanna, where he met his wife—or was she his wife? Maybe Axel was born out of wedlock. There was still so much I didn't know.

As if reading my thoughts, Hanna said, "I can't promise you anything, Lena, but we'll try to find Gunnar's father-in-law's store, if it's still there—you know that's almost thirty-five years ago."

I cleared my throat and said, "Well, I brought a couple of photos, ones my grandmother had. One of them with Gunnar. Maybe someone in the town will recognize him."

Hanna was quiet. As we crisscrossed the country roads, I had the impression we were both lost in thought, maybe in anticipation of what lay ahead.

"We're almost there now, just a short distance," Hanna said as she made an extreme right turn and nearly missed bumping into a tall signpost.

I jumped in my seat, nervous and jittery, wondering what this place where Nazi sympathizers had once lived would be like. The revelation that Gunnar had participated in a local Nazi party just added to my horrors of what I already knew. All of this made me increasingly wary of what additional ghastly family history I would uncover.

I wondered if Johann's wife, Rebecca, had known that Gunnar, her brother-in-law, was a Nazi-sympathizer. Surely, there were rumblings of the war in Sweden that summer. The fact that there was a group of Nazis in the vicinity supporting the German push into Poland didn't shock me. Back home, I had done some research and found out that, though Sweden declared its neutrality at the beginning of the war, some government officials were willing to look the other way when German military came through the country by train, the shortest route to occupied Norway. These Scandinavian countries possessed iron ore, sorely needed for Germany's war machine and both countries benefitted economically from the sale of their natural resources. Did Rebecca die because she knew too much and threatened the local Nazi-sympathizers' underground support of Germany, or did Gunnar kill her with a poison because she was a Jew? Axel had seemed to suggest that Rebecca ingested poisonous mushrooms. Did Grandmother know that? Did Rebecca commit suicide, by eating something poisonous, maybe when she learned her parents and siblings were in the Warsaw Ghetto? The whole thing felt like a huge, dark puzzle—I now possessed some of the pieces, but many were still missing.

As we arrived on the outskirts of Smästad, Hanna slowed the car and seemed to wonder which of two roads that came to a fork she should take, then swerved abruptly to the left.

"Yes, I think the town center is this way. Ya, ya, this is it."

I strained to see ahead. There was a petrol station on the outskirts, and Hanna swung into the station. "Better fill up here so we know we can get back home," she said, and came to a stop by one of the gas tanks. An older man, with a greying beard and red bulbous nose, which suggested to me that he drank a lot, approached us. He wore an old captain's hat and his thinning, longish white hair pushed out from under it. His hat, resembling the one my grandmother used to wear, didn't seem quite the attire for a service-station assistant. He approached the driver's-side window as Hanna rolled it down.

"Hej, what can I do for you ladies?" the man asked.

"Fill the tank, please," said Hanna. "And, while you're doing that, may I ask you a few questions?"

The old Swede looked up as he held the nozzle over the gas tank opening, stroked his beard with his other hand, and finally said, "Depends on the question."

"Well, we're from near Ronneby, not from these parts, and we're looking, or rather my niece visiting from America"—Hanna nodded in my direction—"is looking for a family that once lived here, with the name Furugärd. You wouldn't happen to know them, would you? They may have passed on by now."

The old guy looked suspicious as he glanced in through the driver's-side window over at me. "So, what do you want to know, young lady, about the Furugärds—eh?"

"Well, I think my grandmother who immigrated to America from Sweden may have known them—or rather met them. One of them married her brother and had a baby, her nephew, Adolf."

At the mention of that name, something in the man's facial expression changed—like a dark shadow passing over the moon. "Well, I'm not sure I can help you. When might that have been, that your grandmother visited here?"

"In the summer of 1939," I said.

He chuckled. "Well, well, I was just a smart-aleck teenager then—can't recall much." Then, as if choosing his words carefully, he said, "You know that was before the war—the kids in town began meeting in dark alleys at night. Ya, we had some trouble then."

"What kind of trouble?" I asked with caution.

"Well, the dark truth of the matter is, some of the young men began to display swastikas on their bicycles—even carved them into the sides of wooden sheds and places not so well hidden. Seems they fashioned themselves as helping the Nazis. That kind of trouble. Now, I recall why I recognized the name. Ya." He stroked his beard again, lost in thought. "Pretty Linea Furugärd, the one all the town boys liked, began to hang out not with one of the locals, but with a bit older fella from another place—oh, ya. He was from near Ronneby, I think—Gunnar, I think his name was, ya. Now my old brain is working. He would strut around town in his beige shirt with the swastika displayed on the sleeve, and his tall black leather boots. A bit menacing, he was. Could that be who you are looking for? As I said, the girl's name was Linea."

The old man paused, removed the gasoline nozzel from Hanna's gas tank, screwed the lid back on, and continued. "She passed on about three years ago—Linea, that is. Her *mor* and *far* died several years before that. They all seemed to harbor a dark secret. Her parents didn't let her out of the house much. I remember the town gossip was that the lad from Ronneby got her pregnant. When the war in Europe began, he seemed to have disappeared. He was never seen again in Smästad. His brother, a tall, handsome man, came to town and took the boy. Linea and her family were dirt poor, could hardly make ends meet. I suspect he gave them some money for the boy. Never saw the boy again, nor the far. After that, Linea was rarely seen in public and when she was, people here said she was a bit crazy—sad, it was."

Throughout the man's long discourse, I tried to absorb every detail, while Hanna just stood by the car's window and listened. She fidgeted and seemed nervous, as if waiting for something to be revealed that she didn't want to hear.

"Well, tak, sir. I'll pay now," said Hanna. "You answered our questions and we'll be going on our way. Is there a coffee shop in town?"

"Ya, there is—and with good baked goods as well. Just take the first right and you'll see it on your left, next to the police station. All the *poliser* like to get their coffee there. You might even run into famous Inspector Wallander. He's quite known in these parts."

Hanna got back in the car. "Well, aren't you lucky, Lena?" she said. "You got your answers."

I'm sure my skin turned white with the awareness of what my great-uncle Gunnar had done. Besides being a Nazi, he had gotten a woman pregnant—Adolf's, well, Axel's mother. And now this troubled boy had grown up to be a kind man, not able to talk, to articulate his thoughts, which I suspected were deeper than anyone could tell. I just sat quiet as Hanna proceeded towards the town center. She pulled up in front of the coffee shop the old man at the service station had described. Hanna and I got out and went into the café.

A few policemen, who sat at the far end of the counter, stopped their conversation for a minute and looked at us, then proceeded to talk softly over their coffee, hands around their mugs to keep them warm. From time to time one of them would chuckle.

"We'll sit here," Hanna said as she slid into a booth. The café was decorated for the Christmas holidays with Swedish *dala* horses of red-painted wood covered with green-and-white patterns. Tinsel draped the windows. It was hard for me to imagine this being the season of joy when my thoughts seemed to take me to more somber corners of my brain. But, I thought, now that I know this dark secret about Gunnar, it still didn't tell me why Grandmother screamed at night. Could it just be the memories of when she was a young girl and Gunnar tried to rape her? Mother used to say that her father, Olaf, said Grandmother was always cheerful until after her trip back to Sweden when she started having nightmares in her sleep. I continued going over and over the same facts and felt like I kept running into a wall. Something significant was missing, and I didn't know where to look next.

The waitress brought coffee to the table and poured it into large white porcelain mugs. "Can I get you ladies some pastry?" she asked.

"Ya, gut. Why not? Please bring some of the good sweet buns. Tack," said Hanna.

Hanna took off her hat, coat, and scarf, laid them on the seat next to her, ruffled her hair, and looked at me. "Take off that heavy sweater of yours and your hat, Lena, or you know you'll be cold when you go back out into the freezing cold winter air. Feels like it's going to snow again soon."

As if in slow motion, I took off my knit cap and pulled my thick hand-knitted sweater over my head. I mulled over all that I had just learned while I sipped my coffee and tried to make sense of it.

"Well, you're awfully quiet, Lena. What are you thinking?" asked Hanna.

I felt I had to say something. "Hanna, I appreciate you bringing me here; I know it's been hard for you, I mean, having to reveal things that are associated with your own painful memories."

"Well, no, not exactly mine, but Johann's and your grandmother Helga's. It's true, when Johann married me, I knew I would always be second to his first wife, his true love, Rebecca. I must admit, I almost had the breath knocked out of me when the old petrol-station guy told us about Linea and how tragic her life was once Johann took Axel away from her. I guess we know why—they were poor, and Johann knew he could give

Axel a better life, especially since the boy was not all there between the ears. He probably paid the family plenty."

I winced at Hanna's heartless reference to Axel's disability and Johann's bribe. I knew Axel was smart, more so than Hanna seemed to recognize, and he was also observant. What had he seen as a small boy? Ever since the day Axel led me to Rebecca's and Johann's grave and then to the Viking site, I felt he knew more than Hanna knew happened that night, the night Hanna seemed so afraid to talk about.

The waitress arrived with our plate of pastries, poured a refill of coffee in our mugs, and turned to walk away.

"We'll pay now," Hanna said.

"Please, Hanna," I said, "let me pay. I appreciate all that you are doing to help me, and I want to treat you."

"Well, alright, Lena, tack, that's good of you."

On our way home from our visit to Smästad, I pondered all that had been revealed by the gas-station man. There were still more questions in my mind: what really happened to Gunnar? Did he really die in Germany or somewhere helping the Nazis? Why did Rebecca die so suddenly during the time of Helga's visit? I thought of the mystery as a chessboard, and there seemed to be more moves than I could figure out. My mother and I played chess once in a while; of course, she always won, but I appreciated the complexity of the game. It was as if I was now engaged in an equally complicated game of uncovering the truth, one move at a time.

Chapter 28

A day later, after Hanna and I visited Smästad, I finally had the courage to ask her another question that nagged at me.

"Hanna?"

"Yes, Lena. What?'

"Remember a few days ago, when I was coming out of my room to go downstairs and you exited a door near Johann's bedroom, locked it, and said you had been in the attic to get some things?"

Hanna looked nervous. "Ya, go on—I remember. What is it you want to know now, Lena?"

"I'm wondering why you locked the door and seemed nervous. You didn't have anything in your arms."

I noticed Hanna slip her right hand into her pocket and begin fingering something.

"Lena, because there were just things in the attic that I had to check on. I had to be certain everything was there as Johann had said. You arrived so soon after his death and with the memorial service and all, I had not had time to verify why he wanted me to give you these keys so you could see for yourself what he left behind." As she said this, she withdrew a set of two keys from her apron pocket. "Johann asked me on his dying bed to be sure and let you go to the attic after I gave you the note. I meant to give you his note when you first arrived."

Ah, I thought, I wondered when Hanna would finally give me Johann's note.

Hanna's hands were shaking as she handed me the note she had withdrawn from her other pocket.

I took the folded paper and read it to myself.

Dear great niece, Lena,

I hope this will quell your sleeplessness, and help you understand why my sister, your grandmother, Helga, screamed at night. If I do not live long enough to meet you, my dear, I am sure you are every bit as beautiful inside and out as your grandmother was and your mother, sweet Sofia. I have left something for you. Hanna will be giving it to you. Johann

Hanna held up the keys now, which dangled from a silver ring. There was a fob hanging from it also. It was in the shape of one of the Viking runes, a sign I had seen on the stones at the burial ground, but the meaning of which I did not understand.

My curiosity was heightened. Would Johann's "gift" unlock the mysteries that caused me so much anxiety? Why had I not asked for the note sooner when Hanna first mentioned it? Had she hoped I would forget there was a note from him?

Tears stung my eyes. Embarrassed, Hanna looked

away, down at her lap. We were silent.

Then she spoke softly, almost in a whisper: "After you finish your breakfast, Lena, you can go upstairs, and with the larger of the keys, you can unlock the door to the attic and stay there as long as you wish. There in the attic, you will find an old chest. Open it with the smaller key. Here, take them now and eat."

My hands shook as I reached for the keys. I could tell this was hard for Hanna. I couldn't help but think, not knowing what I would discover in the attic—if only Grandmother had been able to talk about that summer of '39 before she took her own life; if only my mother had known the truth, too, before she died, I would not have to be here now, where a grim truth might be revealed. I looked again at the keys that rested in my hand and wondered about the meaning of the symbol that dangled in front of me.

Hanna and I sat in silence, almost in darkness. The morning was overcast. Little light came in through the kitchen window. There were smells of coffee, fresh baked rolls, and yes, herring in the air—where truth hung over us like a dark cloud.

As anxious as I was to climb the stairs to the attic, to find out the truth, I ate slowly this morning, postponing what I feared would be revealed. I clenched the keys in my hand on my lap as I ate. What was it Joseph had said to me as I boarded the train in Paris?

"Remember, once you have uncovered the truth—the real truth—you can never turn back."

What could he have meant by that? I had pondered it for a long time, as the train inched its way north to this land inhabited for years by my ancestors, and once ruled by the Vikings and their gods. They'd pillaged Europe to evolve into a reserved people, proud and inward.

Would I be wounded by the truth—or freed?

Hanna went about her kitchen chores and said little. When, at last, sleepy-eyed Axel appeared, Hanna announced, "Well, Axel, it's about time you awoke. I have lots of chores for you today. Why don't you eat quickly, and I'll take you outside to show you what we need to do? Lena will be busy with other things."

Axel looked over at me and gave me his broad smile. "Hej, Lena," he said.

I smiled back at Axel and said, "Hej." Then I turned to Hanna and said, "I'll go up to the attic as soon as I finish eating your tasty breakfast, Hanna. Maybe Johann's gift will give me some answers I've been seeking."

Hanna looked away, twisting a kitchen towel in her hands. Then she turned abruptly and walked out of the kitchen, turning back for a minute to say, "Come on, Axel. We have chores to do."

Axel looked back at me with a puzzled expression as he followed Hanna out of the kitchen, down the hall, and out to the mud porch, where I saw them put on their warm coats and hats and walk out the door.

I had not seen Hanna this distraught since my arrival.

• • •

A half hour later, in the quiet and empty house, I walked slowly down the hall from the kitchen, mounted the stairs, and walked towards the door to the attic, the one from which Hanna had emerged two days before. My hands trembled as I slipped the key into the lock and turned the door handle. It opened with ease and there before me lay a long stairway to the attic. I mounted the stairs. As I arrived at the top, I remembered I had forgotten to ask Hanna in what part of the attic was the chest that Uncle Johann had wanted me to open. I stumbled over a stack of old magazines and books, looked around in the semi-darkness until my eyes had adjusted. I found a switch for a light bulb that hung down in the center of the attic ceiling and switched it on.

I whispered to myself, "That's better." I walked slowly around the attic, being careful not to bump my head, as it nearly touched the steeply sloped eves. I was amazed at the array of objects I found there: an old gilded bird cage, an ancient sewing machine, more stacks of books and magazines, even a dollhouse. That must have been something that Helga played with as a child. There were stacks of old sheet music, too—probably Rebecca and Johann's. Hanna had said Johann didn't have the heart to play his violin much after Rebecca died and Helga returned to America.

As my eyes adjusted to the dim light, they fell on a large, old, carved wooden chest in a dark corner of the attic. As I made my way to the chest, I coughed from the dust my feet kicked up. Finally, I kneeled down in front of the object of my search. I wiped a thick layer of dust off the top to behold two letters, JP, carved into the lid of the trunk. They were surrounded by Nordic motifs. I wondered if my great-grandfather had carved those. JP surely stood for Johann Pettersson, my great-grandfather's name, Grandmother and Johann's father.

I reached into the pocket of my blue jeans and pulled out the key ring again, looking to make sure that I had the smaller of the two keys, and slipped it in the lock. It went in easily. I took a deep breath, turned the key, heard it click, then I slowly lifted the lid of the chest. It was heavy, and I had to stand to get more leverage as I pushed the lid up and looked down into the chest's contents. I gasped.

There in front of my gaze were two large black leather boots, somewhat scuffed, lying on top of some old newspapers. I reached down and lifted the boots out—strange, I thought, how the sides looked scraped, as if they were dragged through gravel or over stones. Then I carefully took out the newspapers, which were yellowed and fragile, torn in places. I noticed that the one at the top displayed a photo of a group of men—again I gasped, for the men all wore Nazi uniforms and tall black boots. I had often seen photos like this in old newsreels that Mr. Christiansen had shown our class. I also remembered pictures like these of men with the same gesture, hands raised in the sign of Heil Hitler. I looked closer. There, in the center of the front row, was a face someone had circled in red—a face I recognized from my grandmother's photos. I could read his name in tiny print under the photo. Gunnar Petersson. Who had circled his face? I thought it was probably Johann. Under the newspaper, which I laid on the floor beside the boots, was a uniform folded neatly with the sleeves displaying the Swastika face up. I dug under the uniform, and my hands touched the corner of what I thought was an envelope. I pulled it out, and yes, it was an envelope with my name on the outside written in neat script, the same handwriting I had seen on Johann's note. The manila envelope was tightly sealed with tape and what appeared to be glue. If anyone had tampered with it, it would have been obvious. Maybe Hanna had not tried or if she did, she realized surely that her efforts would be seen. She must be wondering now, with some trepidation, I thought, what I would find in that envelope. Would the truth be damaging to her?

I tore open the envelope in slow motion, pulled out what was obviously a letter, a long one, and began to read it:

Dear great niece, Lena,

If you are reading this letter, I have unfortunately died before we could meet in person. It was my hope that I could see you before passing and that I could explain the circumstances I think you are in search of, circumstances that might be the cause of your Grandmother Helga's screams at night. So, this is, I must tell you, my letter of confession of something I held within for nearly thirty-five years. Please sit down. This may be hard for you to read but I must bare my soul before I die and rid myself of this sin in the eyes of our almighty God.

When your grandmother arrived with her three-year-old Sofia in her arms and stepped off the ship's exit plank, Rebecca, my beautiful wife, and I were there to meet her with open arms. It was the Summer of 1939. We did know that Hitler was threatening to conquer all of Europe, to rid Germany and all countries of Jews, to make way for the perfect Aryan race. In fact, he thought we Swedes were the purest race of all. The parents of my beautiful wife, Rebecca, were anxious when we announced we wanted to marry during my visit with them in Poland, in 1936. They were happy for us and asked me to take Rebecca back to Sweden. We didn't realize what they already knew, that Hitler would capture Poland and send its Jews to concentration camps. Actually, many Jews put their children on ships bound for Denmark, to where they thought they would be safer. Rebecca's family did the same with her younger sister, then only twelve. When Rebecca and I returned to Sweden, she spent anxious time trying to locate that sister, Suzanna, without success.

When Helga arrived with little Sofia, to visit us, we tried to put all that aside. We spent lovely evenings around the parlor, Rebecca and I playing our violins, Rebecca singing. For the first couple of weeks we were all delirious with happiness. The only dark side was that Gunnar, my brother, refused to join us. He never liked Rebecca and was not that anxious to confront our sister, Helga, and her child. She had emigrated when he was nineteen and as far as he was concerned, she was out of his life. I remember that Helga felt somewhat sad about that but at the same time, she held a certain fear of him. Gunnar was gone often for days at a time in the village of Smästad, where he had fallen for a woman from a poor family.

We were to learn just before Helga arrived that Gunnar was involved with a growing Nazi movement in this southern part of Sweden. There was a rather large group of Nazi sympathizers in that village. It was not far by train from Kristianstad, where many Nazis arrived on trains on their way to Norway and some trains were shipping the iron ore, so needed for their military weaponry. Apparently, Gunnar was popular with the *group and gained a leadership role. In the meantime, Göring, Hitler's right-hand man, had established a house here in Sweden, his vacation house, not far from here. He liked our Swedish women.*

Gunnar hoped to impress Göring. Once I knew of Gunnar's involvement with the Nazi sympathizers, I worried constantly that he would do something to Rebecca. Perhaps he would tell Göring about my Jewish wife. I was distraught with fear but did not want to ruin Helga's visit with us. One day Rebecca began to complain of stomach pains. She hoped and thought she might be pregnant. We had tried to have a child for several years without luck. The pains did not let up and we had made an appointment to see the doctor in Ronneby, but she collapsed very suddenly the night before her appointment. We called the doctor, but he arrived too late. Everyone who knew Gunnar was a Nazi leader in the neighboring community assumed, as I knew they might, it had been Gunnar who had poisoned Rebecca. An autopsy revealed that indeed Rebecca had been poisoned from a very toxic mushroom which grows in our forest. If one ingests the whole thing at once, death is almost instant, but if just a little bit is put into one's food or tea, a little at a time, it produces sickness and eventually kills. My sister, Helga—your grandmother—was convinced, too, that it had been Gunnar who poisoned Rebecca with his hatred of Jews. We buried Rebecca on our property in the forest. Helga was distraught and almost inconsolable. She and Rebecca had established a friendship during her visit. Helga had always wished she had a sister.

One day, a week after Rebecca's funeral and burial, I

was in the shed by the field. I smelled the sickening sweet smell of the toxic mushrooms. I rarely went in there—it was Gunnar who always did the farming, like our mother. I was looking for something that Hanna needed. She sent me out there to fetch it. I smelled that odor from the poisonous mushrooms and then saw Gunnar's work apron on the hook by the door, from whence the smell seemed to be coming. Sure enough, in the pocket of the apron, I found small particles of the poisonous mushrooms. Your grandmother came out looking for me. I was nearly delirious with this proof that Gunnar, our own brother, had murdered my beautiful wife, Rebecca. At that very moment I could see Gunnar was in the field digging up potatoes. As I peered out at him, I knew I had to do something, something horrible. Your grandmother tried to stop me, but I was overcome with rage, and grabbed a shovel and took off across the field. I have to stop here for a moment, Lena. I am wracked with grief and shame at what I did and believe this is why I am now dying. It's God's punishment.

It was over in a minute. I will never forget Helga's screams—as she tried to stop me. I struck Gunnar's head with the shovel and he toppled to the ground dead. I suspect, Lena, that the screams I heard from my sister are what you suffered from hearing all those years she lived with you and your mother.

My hands were trembling as I clutched at the letter and gasped at the truth. Then the tears came, sobs that had been pent up in me ever since my grandmother's suicide and my mother's premature death. I felt the warm tears flow down my cheeks and couldn't stop them from coming as they dripped onto Johann's letter and the ink began to run. I quickly wiped the paper with my shirt sleeve and took a deep breath. I could see there was more to the letter, but I could barely go on. I leaned back on my heels. How could this be true? How could Grandmother have watched her beloved brother, Johann, her favorite brother, murder their brother Gunnar? How? No wonder Grandmother could never look at his photo without it bringing back this earth-shattering memory. It was like a scene from Hamlet.

The letter from Johann went on. I had to change my position—my legs under me were beginning to cramp. I moved around and leaned against the chest, legs outstretched in front of me, to read on:

I did a terrible thing, Lena. Not only did I kill my brother, I convinced Helga to help me bury him. She, of course, realized that Gunnar had poisoned Rebecca, the sister she had just begun to love. We buried Gunnar at the runes; I knew no one would ever dig up that sacred spot. I lied to Gunnar's woman friend, the mother of Adolf, that Gunnar went off to Germany to fight in Hitler's army. I offered to raise Adolf. As they were very poor and she was sickly, the family agreed. Adolf never knew, I don't think, what happened to his father. I changed Adolf's name to Axel to erase the terrible reminder of his father's Nazi activities.

I gasped again, choked back a sob, and had to wipe the tears again with the back of my shirt sleeve to go on reading.

So that is my story, Lena, that is why your grandmother

screamed and I suffered for the rest of my life knowing not only what I did to my brother, but what I did to my sister who could no longer stand the memory of that night and walked into the sea.

I am gone now and perhaps my soul is burning in Hell, but I feel relieved to have finally confessed this. Even Hanna does not know the whole story. She only knows of the death of Rebecca. For a long time, she stayed away from the house, but I needed someone to help with the housekeeping and raising of Axel whom I've loved deeply all these years. She has accepted the lie, since we decided to marry, that I was raising Axel because Gunnar ran off, never to be seen again.

I hope this will free you from your nights of sleeplessness, knowing the truth of your grandmother's screams. My confession is my only redemption.

Your loving Great Uncle Johann

I looked up from the letter and under my breath whispered, "Oh, so that's why Axel lay down on the ground at the Viking burial ground. He knows—somehow, he knows—his father is buried there, but how?"

After a long while, I folded the letter and returned it to its envelope, then laid it in the chest and returned all the other items back to their resting place. I would have no need of them—they only held dark and terrible truths. I stayed there for a long while, finally realizing that the light bulb, which I had switched on, had begun to flicker. It would soon be very dark. I told myself it was time to leave. I rose, walked to the steps, descended them, then closed the door and locked it. I would never have to go there again.

Chapter 29

I lay down on my bed, closed my eyes, hoping to close out the ghastly truth of what my grandmother had done, but only saw images of that horrible event on that terrifying day in 1939—the day that changed her life and affected my mother's and mine too. I knew I would have to move on, forget, and make sure my own child, if I were ever to have one, would not be hindered by this dark family history.

In a short while, I heard the downstairs door open and voices of Hanna and Axel. They were home, and I would have to face them with what I knew, at least Hanna. Before I could confront her, though, I had to write Joseph to tell him that I now knew the secret of why my grandmother was so haunted, but that before I could return to Paris, there were still a few loose ends I had to figure out. I paused to ponder how Axel could know his father was buried at the runes; how could that be when Johann and Hanna had told him Gunnar had gone off to fight in the war in Europe, never to return. I had to figure out this one last piece of the puzzle before

I could rest in peace and try to accept this tragic truth in my family—that a great-uncle was a Nazi and that my grandmother and her brother murdered him.

Still shaken by the day's events and what I had found out, I finally descended the stairs. I could hear voices in the kitchen and found Hanna there with her friend Astrid. They were having coffee and talking about a local district politician and how disgusting he was. Hanna looked up and Astrid stopped talking. Hanna had a strange expression on her face, not of fear but ambiguity.

"Oh, excuse me. I didn't mean to interrupt you," I said. "Please go on with your conversation."

"Lena, we were just finishing, Hanna said. Astrid has to go home to be with her family now."

"Ya, Lena, I was just telling Hanna, I have to leave. It was a good day for us, wasn't it, Hanna?"

"Ya, it was."

It was obvious to me that Hanna had kept her secret, even from her best friend, maybe too ashamed to disclose this dark mark on her family, on my family.

"Where's Axel?" I asked, missing his usual presence.

"Oh, I think he's out feeding the goats," said Hanna. "Astrid, could you tell him to come in for some supper now?"

"Most certainly. Good night, Lena; good night, Hanna. I'll see you at sewing club next week. We're making the Yule decorations. Don't forget."

"Oh, I won't. Maybe Lena would like to come along."

"Oh, do bring her along."

Astrid strode down the hall where she donned her

coat and hat on the mud porch, and I heard the door close.

Hanna looked down at her hands, clinched into tight fists in her lap—waiting. An awkward silence filled the kitchen with its heavy presence. Then, finally, Hanna looked up and said, "Lena, I imagine you're hungry. You look pale. Are you okay?"

"Yes, Hanna, but Uncle Johann's letter was a shock. A big one."

Hanna's expression changed, like a windshield wiper had passed across it. She stared at me as if trying to decipher code, to understand what I was saying, what I knew.

"Well, yes, I guess you found the chest and saw the newspaper photo of Gunnar with his Nazi friends. Ya, I imagined that would be a shock, but something you already knew. What else did you discover? What letter?" It was clear she was nervous, not knowing what else Johann may have revealed.

I realized that Hanna did not know about the letter in the chest. She apparently had just hastily checked its top contents, when she heard me downstairs and came down to meet me.

Hanna continued, "You mean he told you about Gunnar in the Nazi party and how he died when he went off to fight in the war. Is that what you mean, Lena?"

"No, no, I didn't mean that," I said. "I mean the part about Rebecca dying from poisonous mushrooms." I paused. "Go on, Lena," Hanna said. Her faced turned pale, and I noticed her hands start to tremble.

"Well, it was very sad to hear about Rebecca dying in such a tragic way—poisoned!" I waited.

Hanna looked nervous. "I didn't know that, Lena.

Johann never told me. We didn't have an autopsy, but I suspected she had been poisoned by something she ate—well, I mean she complained of severe stomach pains. Did Johann tell you about the day in the field when he ran from the shed?"

"No. Can you tell me about that, Hanna?" I asked.

I sensed that Hanna was groping now. She wasn't sure what or how much I knew.

My mind was working on overtime now, trying to put together this last piece of the puzzle: evidently, she had watched the murder of Gunnar that day from the kitchen window. She had alluded earlier that she heard a scream, that she watched something from the window, and then remembered how Johann came into the house very upset and how he later left at night and Grandmother followed. They had something to do, she said, but she could not figure out what. She knew. She had lied. She knew, too, about the autopsy, but hoped that Johann hadn't revealed that in his letter to me.

"Well, I always suspected that Rebecca died from eating poisonous mushrooms," said Hanna. "She wasn't a very good cook, so I did most of the cooking for them. She didn't know how to identify the good mushrooms from the bad like I did—well, I mean, she may have put them in her food without knowing.

I knew she was casting about for something to say that would not incriminate her. What was she trying to cover up? What was her real role in all of this? She loved Johann; she told me that herself.

She rose now from her chair and moved nervously towards the door, like a trapped fox, trying to break free from the trap. But why, why would she have something to hide?

A light bulb went on in my head and without thinking further, I blurted out, "Did you put the poisonous mushrooms in Rebecca's food, Hanna, because you wanted Johann?"

Hanna's eyes opened wide, and she looked as if she had seen a ghost—her hands twisted her apron and her skin glistened with sweat. Dumbfounded, she could not open her mouth but, instead, started to walk out of the room, down the hall towards the front door.

"No, wait, Hanna." I followed her down the hall, and just then Axel walked in through the door; Hanna turned into the parlor with the look of someone caught in a snare. Axel looked bewildered. The two of us followed Hanna, who collapsed on the settee in sobs."

"Ya, Lena, you never would understand. Ya, I loved Johann more than anyone in the world, more even than his sister, your grandmother Helga, but all I was to him, as long as Rebecca, his Jewish beauty, was alive, was a maid, a lowly maid. Ya, it was I who poisoned Rebecca."

Axel stood frozen in place, with a soulful look in his eyes, not really understanding the English Hanna spoke, but he knew something was terribly wrong. He looked up at me with questioning eyes, then reached down to pat Hanna's back. "OK, OK, Mamma," was all he could mutter.

At first, I just stood there in shock, still trying to put it all together, another revelation, as if the ones I read in Johann's letter were not enough.

"But, Hanna, why then did Johann think it was Gunnar?" I looked up at Axel, whose eyes grew wide and watery with tears hearing his father's name. Of course, he did not understand my question but could tell this was a conversation of serious consequence. "Why did he kill his own brother and bury him, with my grandmother's help, at the Viking burial ground on the hill?" It was all making sense even as I asked the question.

Sniffling and blowing her nose in her apron, Hanna looked up with bloodshot eyes and a pleading look. "Don't you see, Lena, I had to kill Rebecca to have Johann, but then I had to make sure he would love me. I knew he would need my help if he had to raise Axel. So, I had to figure out how Gunnar would disappear." She turned to Axel and switched to Swedish: "You know, don't you, my sweet adopted son, your father went off to war, and your uncle Johann and I had to raise you, right?"

Axel looked up at me, confused, and tried to talk, to tell all he knew but could not; only blubbering sounds came out of his mouth, and he ran to the door and left the house.

"See what you've done, Lena—you've scared Axel."

Hanna went on, "Johann, Axel, and me, we were very happy for many years. No one had to know. Johann came to love me and need me. We were married, and Axel was like our own son." Hanna paused, her head in her hands, then looked up, her face tear-stained. "Ya, I was horrified," she said, "when I saw Johann, my gentle violin player, run from the shed where I had planted the mushrooms in Gunnar's work apron—run and strike Gunnar on the head, but it was too late. I couldn't stop him, and your grandmother couldn't either."

I sat down in the big armchair and just stared into space, still in shock. It was Hanna who had planted the mushrooms in Gunnar's apron. Gunnar was innocent.

He did not kill Rebecca—Hanna did, and she was re-sponsible, too, for the death of Gunnar. How could I deal with this—what should I do? I just looked at Hanna as she whimpered like an injured animal and curled into herself on the couch, crying.

And what about Axel? How did he know all along his father was buried at the Viking stones, that he had not died in the war?

Hanna began to talk again, finally, quietly, her voice barely a whisper, raspy from her crying. Perhaps she sought the relief of confession. "After many years," she said, "I told Axel that Johann had lied to him, that he loved him so much he did not want him to think of his father as a Nazi; Axel thinks that Gunnar became very ill and that his uncle Johann buried him at the Viking burial site to honor his memory and also, so he would be near us. Axel believed him and grew up a happy child, loved by me and Johann. What is wrong with that, Lena?"

I didn't know how to reply to the twisted rationale Hanna presented for her two crimes and lies to Axel. At the same time, I understood that she had played an important role in Axel's life, that it would do no good for her to be taken away from him now, to be tried in a court and to go to prison for the rest of her life.

"I have to go upstairs to think, Hanna. You have confessed, and now I know why my grandmother screamed at night and what happened to Rebecca. Even she believed, as Johann did, that as horrible as it was, what her brother and she had done to their brother was justified because Gunnar had poisoned Rebecca. Thank goodness she never knew the truth, that it was you who poisoned Rebecca and then pointed the finger at Gunnar." It might not have changed her fear and hatred of Gunnar, but it would have given her even more trauma that she had assisted in the killing, or at least burial of her brother for the wrong reason.

Hanna, still sniffling, her eyes swollen and red, looked up at me now and asked, "What will you do, Lena? Will they take me away? What will Axel do?"

"That is what I have to think about now. Please stay here while I go upstairs. I trust that you will not attempt to flee; I know how important you and Axel are to one another."

Hanna just resumed her fetal position on the couch and began to rock back and forth.

I dragged myself upstairs and into my room where I sat on the bed and tried to think. I felt almost panicky at first and desperate to talk to Joseph. But I could not call him now. He would be asleep. This was my decision to make. If I called the police and they took Hanna away, the crime, even if they could prove it, had been committed so many years ago, how could Hanna be put away? Also, she may not confess to the crime and it would be my word—a young American girl's, a distant relative's—against hers, that of a stalwart community member in a small town in Skåne. If they did believe me and Hanna was forced to waste away in a Swedish prison, what then would happen to Axel? He loved her and they took good care of each other on this farm. Just as I was trying to work out the right response to this terrible crime of lies and deception, I heard Axel downstairs calling out my name, "Lena, Lena . . ." I ran out of my room and looked down in the hallway at his frightened face, contorted and pointing at the door, trying somehow to tell me something, something important.

I ran down the stairs and followed him outside into the cold and dank late afternoon. It was nearly dark. He motioned for me to follow him as he ran towards the pond.

I stopped a moment in shock when I saw what he saw. There on the gravel at the edge of the pond were Hanna's two shoes. We looked out just in time to see her slowly walking into the deep water, her shoulders barely visible. Without hesitation Axel pulled off his jacket and shoes and ran into the water, swimming as fast as he could. He reached Hanna just as her head went under. He put his arm around her upper torso and swam with her back to shore where I waited with my sweater and his jacket to quickly wrap around her shivering body. With her arms draped over our necks, we dragged Hanna, limp and wet, back to the house. We had arrived just in time—to prevent another suicide.

We put Hanna into her bed, forced her to drink some hot tea, and Axel began to hum a beautiful lullaby. I walked quietly out, leaving the two of them alone. Then, in my room, I lay down on my bed, still shaken from all that had happened in the last twenty-four hours: my discovery of the contents of the chest in the attic, Johann's letter explaining the murder of his brother Gunnar, and the part that Helga had played in their brother's burial. Then had come the admission of guilt by Hanna for what had seemed at first the unexplainable death of Rebecca, the woman so loved by my grandmother, and lastly, the near suicide by Hanna. It was almost more than one soul could handle. Now I had to decide what my next actions would be. I asked myself, in a whisper, "What do I usually do when I am upset or up against some kind of problem?" I grabbed my journal and my beloved bright green fountain pen, the one Grandmother Helga had given me so many years ago and began to write. I knew I had to turn my grief about Grandmother's secrets into the best-ever novel I could write, the kind of writing Mrs. Olsen had always encouraged me to do. I'd start with a prologue, like this:

"On that late summer day, the sun hung low in the sky, shadows of clouds danced across a rippled field where a man bent to dig up potatoes and sugar beets. Two figures, a man and a woman, emerged from a blood-red shed on the edge of the field. The towheaded man carried a steel shovel and ran towards the other crouched in the field, head bent as he dug. The woman ran after, screaming something to the running man. It was too late. He brought the shovel down hard over the head of the crouched man, who toppled to the earth. It was done. The woman stopped in her tracks, slumped to the ground, her hand to her mouth. The towheaded man, who had been running, dropped the shovel, fell with his head in his hands. The earth seemed to tremble, but there was only silence, no sound. No sound of the breeze tangled in the birch leaves, no cow's moos, no human cries. All was mute. The sun slipped behind a cloud. Dusk arrived.

Three hours later, the moon was high enough to light their way. The towheaded man was covered in mud, his boots bloodstained. The woman's apron was splotched with blood. The two dragged a tarp with the limp body from the red shed to the nearby lake, its waters still and dark, algae floating on top. They looked at the rowboat, once blue but now scraped down to bare wood, tied to the slumping pier. Pine paddles rested in its bough. The man and the woman stopped, their shoulders pulled down by the weight of the body, arms strained. The man, lost in thought for a moment, looked out over the lake. 'No, wait,' he said, his voice hoarse. 'They'll dredge the lake. We can't bury him here.' Still holding onto the heavy tarp, with one hand the woman lifted the corner of her apron to wipe the sweat from her brow. 'Well, then, where?' She glanced in the direction of the hill, a few hundred feet away, shrouded in the darkness where the birch and the ash grew, and the stones stood.

'There,' the man said as he pointed to the same hill. The place of the stones with the runes. We'll bury him deep; they won't dare disturb an ancient Viking burial ground.' They pulled the body behind them. The boots of the dead man, still on, made scraping sounds on the pebbles that rimmed the lake as they dragged the body toward the hill.

'What have we done?' she cried softly under her heavy breathing.

'Don't worry. We'll finish it and then forget it—all of it—and go on,' said the man. They stopped from time to time to catch their breaths. The woman shivered and they went on. Soon, autumn leaves would hide the ground where they walked. Geese would fly south. Snow would come. There would be no trace of their digging and she would be gone, back to America— never again to return to her homeland."

Finally, as night came and outside the moon rose in the sky, I set down my pen, tired. I knew now what

I had to do. It wouldn't be right to call the authorities, accuse Hanna of murder, a murder that took place over thirty-five years ago, leaving Axel without the care and affection that Hanna gave him. Who would gain from this action? No one. Grandmother was dead. She had taken her secrets with her, fortunately never knowing the truth about Hanna's love for her brother, the jealousy that had motivated her to poison by mushrooms Johann's beloved Rebecca. Certainly, Mother, now gone, too, wouldn't have anything to say.

I set my journal aside, rose from the bed, and walked to Hanna's room, which was now dark with just a sliver of moonlight coming through the lace curtains of her bedroom window. Hanna had fallen asleep with Axel's jacket still around her. She snored quietly. Axel lay on the floor next to her, covered with an old afghan. The two looked peaceful. I knew I had made the right decision. Tomorrow I would call Peter and tell him I was staying for another week for the celebration of Christmas with Hanna and Axel. Then I would be leaving the day after to take the train back to Paris. Would Peter be able to join me? Down deep, I hoped so.

The End

EPILOGUE

A few days later, Lena Larsson scattered the ashes of her mother and grandmother next to the graves of Rebecca and Johann in Blekinge woods. The day after the Yule celebrations, she returned to Paris on a train with her friend, Peter, hopeful that Joseph would be there to meet her. She hoped she would now sleep more peacefully, having learned the truth, the effects on just one family, amongst many, of the horrible acts of Adolf Hitler and the Nazis, including the erasure of millions of innocent people in concentration camps throughout Europe. She knew his dark imprint on the world should never be forgotten. She would write about it.

ACKNOWLEDGEMENTS

Although it has taken me nearly eight years to write this story, first inspired by one of my visits with cousins in Sweden, it has been a labor of love. I could not have accomplished this without the support of my dear husband who took undue care to keep us stocked up on groceries, cooked many meals and was there to read and offer suggestions along the way. Thanks also go to my two daughters for their encouragement to pursue this story. My daughter, Dawn Evans, was a phone call away throughout my writing, encouraging me and even doing some early editing.

I owe thanks to my cousin Torkel Mollerström in Sweden, whose father, Boris, now deceased, first inspired the story with a comment he made about Sweden during World War II. Torkel also kindly supplied the photo taken in the Blekinje woods for my cover. Thanks to Aaron Vasquez who helped with the cover and Lacy Rasmussen, my model.

Thanks to my developmental editors Merilyn Simonds, Andrea Hurst, Dale Griffiths Stamos and Karen Fisher, who read some of the first drafts and encouraged me to continue working on the story. My gratitude also goes to dear friends, Rosalie Hewins, Catherine Matthias and to Kate Fisher (no relation to Karen Fisher) who read early drafts and gave me enthusiastic support throughout my writing journey. Lastly, big thank you to my copy editor, Frances Wood, for her thorough attention to my manuscript.

I am grateful for all of the writing teachers with whom I have studied for the last fifteen years at Summer Fishtrap in Joseph, Oregon and with the San Miguel de Allende Literary Sala and Conference in Mexico. Amongst those who had the greatest influence on my writing development are Liz Prato, Luis Alberto Urrea, Dinty Moore, Dale Griffiths Stamos, and Elizabeth Rosner, whose book *Survivor Café* I have quoted on the cover page. There have been many others, whose names I cannot remember, who helped me hone my writing skills. For all of them, I am thankful. Indeed, it has been a long journey.

BIBLIOGRAPHY OF
RESEARCH SOURCES

Books:

Hitler's Scandinavian Legacy by John Gilmour and Jill Stephenson
Survivor Café by Elizabeth Rosner
Deep River by Karl Marlantes
Clatsop County Historical Society Quarterly CUMTEX

and

Conversations with a Jungian Psychologist Susan E. Schwartz, about the
Absent Father Effect on Daughters: Father Desire, Father Wounds

BOOK GROUP GUIDE

Questions about Dark Secrets

1. What impacted you most by the Prologue?

2. Does the author give you a sense of the time and place the action in the Prologue takes place?

3. What in the descriptions of Lena and the "all woman household" struck you the most?

4. Is Lena a sympathetic character? How about her mother, Sofia, and her grandmother, Helga?

5. Which characters(s) in the story, did you empathize with the most? For what reasons?

6. Did the author's descriptions of Astoria, Paris, and southern Sweden seem real; did you get a sense of each place?

7. Who was your favorite character? Explain why.

8. Were you surprised to learn some historical facts about Sweden during the time of WWII you might not have known before?

9. Did it inspire you to want to know more?

10. Was the ending a surprise?

Would you like to read more about Lena and her journey as a writer, her romance with Joseph, and or with Peter? Will she succeed as a writer? Tell the author.

Please contact the author, Sher Davidson at her website https://sherdavidson.com
To set up an in-person visit with your book club or via Zoom.